THE SECRET OF TELFAIR INN

For Erik in
appreciation for reading
my book ———

Idella Bodie

Illustrations

By LOUISE YANCEY

THE SECRET OF TELFAIR INN

By IDELLA BODIE

SANDLAPPER
PUBLISHING, INC.
ORANGEBURG,
SOUTH CAROLINA

First Paperbound Edition 1983

Copyright © 1971 by Sandlapper Publishing Co., Inc.

ISBN: 0-87844-050-X

Library of Congress Catalog Card Number: 799-177909

Published by Sandlapper Publishing Co., Inc.
P.O. Box 1932, Orangeburg, S.C. 29116-1932
Manufactured in the United States of America

To Beth and John,
who were always curious about old houses

Although there is an old inn in Aiken which kindled the spark for this story, the facts in the story concerning it are purely fictional, as are the characters of the book. The historical facts and places are true and have been well researched in the Aiken County Public Library and the Minnie B. Kennedy Junior High School Library.

Idella Bodie

Contents

THE SECRET OF TELFAIR INN

1.

The Dixie Way

"Way down South in Dixie!" sang Phil as the Dunlaps' station wagon sped down the Dixie Highway.

"Hurray! Hurray!" chimed in his younger sister Marcy.

Two weeks ago when Mr. Dunlap had announced that the Northern university where he taught wanted him to go to South Carolina for historical research, the red-haired Dunlap children hadn't been so jubilant. They had loved the short trips they'd made with him before, but *the whole summer*! That was something else.

"Gee, Dad," Phil had said, "that'll mean the relay team'll have a missing link."

"Yes, I know, son," his father had answered sympathetically.

"Now, Philip," Mrs. Dunlap cut in, "your father's so pleased to be asked to do this for the university. It's quite an honor." And with her martyred expression she added, "We

1

don't want to spoil it for him, now do we?"

Watching Phil's freckled brow furrow under his mop of red hair, Marcy knew what he must be thinking. They'd been proud of Phil's agility on the track team. Last year as a sixth grader he'd helped set records. The summer fitness program was important.

Marcy was always good for an idea, and as usual she had one. "I know—Phil could stay with Aunt Grace." As quickly as the words left her mouth she was sorry. Who would she play with if Phil stayed behind? If there wasn't anyone else around, her older brother would condescend to play with her. In an attempt to take back her idea, she said, "At least Phil doesn't have a best friend to leave the way I do. Ellen and I have been best friends since third grade, and in August we'll be eleven together and I won't be here." She pursed her lips, running the freckles along her nose together. The months ahead had been bright with promise, and now all the things they'd planned would be impossible.

Both the Dunlap children had red hair and freckles like their father, but Phil's eyes were brown and Marcy's were kitten grey. Although Philip didn't like to admit it, many of their interests were similar too. Even ballet, piano and sewing lessons had failed to dampen Marcy's tomboyish streak. The opportunity for adventure always put a twinkle in her grey eyes.

In spite of the ties that must be severed for the summer, Marcy and Phil had found it exciting when Dad got out the road map to trace their journey southward. Time had rushed to the date they set for departure, and now the Dunlaps were riding for the second long day to reach their destination. As the road unfolded behind them, Phil and Marcy jumped at every chance to climb from their seats between Dad's books and Mom's fresh linens and stretch their legs. And now, fidgety with the excitement of seeing their summer home for the first time, their restlessness soared.

"Hey, Dad, that sign said, 'Aiken—2 miles,' " Phil yelled.

"Oh, look!" exclaimed Mrs. Dunlap. "There are some magnolias—and in bloom, too. Those creamy-white blossoms make georgeous arrangements, but you can't touch them, you know. It yellows them."

Tom Dunlap smiled at his wife, and Marcy knew he must be thinking what a flower lover she was. Then he said, "Aiken is noted for its lovely trees and gardens. It's a small resort town, you know." Actually Mr. Dunlap had told them very little about what the town was like, but he had said the furnished apartment they were to live in used to be a fashionable inn years ago.

"Scores of famous people have lived in Aiken," Mr. Dunlap continued. "Many of the old mansions have been left to schools and churches there now, but of course some wealthy winter residents do still come."

"Hey, that's funny," said Phil. "They go north for the summer and we come south." A groan trailed off reminding them he'd not forgotten what he had left behind.

This mood left him as quickly as he noticed the name of the highway they had turned onto. "Whiskey Road?" he read incredulously.

"What an intriguing name," his mother said. "There must be a story behind that, Tom." And then, "Oh, look at that lovely serpentine wall with the ivy trailing over it."

"Say," cried Marcy, "there's a door in it like the one the camel couldn't get through."

Mr. Dunlap slowed the car, and they all drank in the scenery. The streets were wide and there wasn't much traffic

3

at all. Late afternoon sunlight splattered through the giant magnolias and oaks whose hanging branches made an arch over their car. Azaleas flanked the roadside.

"It's such a lovely town!" Mrs. Dunlap's youthful face reflected her inner happiness.

"Let's see," her husband mused as he approached a traffic light, "a left here and follow the road to the wooden bridge, the realtor's letter said. It's called old Telfair Inn." They turned left onto another shady road that wound down a steep hill.

"Those look like stables," Mrs. Dunlap commented, pointing out of her husband's window.

"Yes, Aiken is famous for horses, too," Mr. Dunlap explained. He was intent now on directions the realtor had mailed him.

On Marcy's side there was a forest of gnarled old magnolias. It was thick with an impassable undergrowth of low-hanging limbs and vines that twisted and turned right up to the edge of the road.

"It must be just ahead," Mr. Dunlap said as he began the ascent from the valley the road had drawn them into. "Yes, this is it. He said there was construction going on across the street—a complex of modern apartments."

"And there's the wooden bridge just ahead," Mrs. Dunlap added, smoothing her soft chestnut hair.

From the back seat Marcy and Phil were straining for all they were worth to see ahead. As the car broke from the shade, Marcy couldn't believe her eyes—through the windshield she saw what might have been a mansion in its day. The front of the building with its tall columns was freshly painted, but a distance beyond Marcy could see that much of the huge, rambling old inn now lay in dilapidated ruins.

Leaning low in the car, Phil could see the irregular roof line of the many-gabled house. "Wow! Look at those lightning rods!" he cried. Countless aged chimneys jutted skyward.

In spite of the enormous size of the inn there was little yard, and when Mr. Dunlap stopped the car it was very near the wooden bridge and the entrance to the inn. Before anyone could say "boo," Phil sprang from the car. "Gol-ly!" he shouted, running through bamboo that thinly hedged a gigantic ravine.

In seconds Marcy was behind him. "Willikins!" she cried, and way down in the bottom of the gorge a tiny voice said, "Willikins!"

"Philip! Marcia! Come with us," their mother called as she climbed the steps to the veranda.

They pulled themselves away from the ravine with its mysterious vines hanging in great ropes and followed their parents into the entrance hall of the inn.

"Dad," Marcy said, pulling at her father's arm, "you gotta see—"

"Just a minute, Marcy; one thing at a time. Let's find out who's in charge here."

The four of them stood there straining to see in the dimness of the great hallway. There was no light in the room except through the screen door they had just entered. Late evening shadows mixed with the deep wine color of the carpet and reflected a crimson eeriness around them. The mood was repeated in the ornately-framed mirror above a massively carved chest. Five dark doorways with heavy locks opened off the hallway. The stillness of the high-ceilinged hall engulfed them.

Marcy felt a shiver down her spine and edged closer to her father.

5

2.
Silas Crowe

From somewhere behind a wall there was the creaking of boards as if someone were walking up stairs. A key clicked from the other side of a door at the end of the long hallway. The doorknob turned. The four Dunlaps waited expectantly as the door creaked open.

Suddenly an old, stoop-shouldered man, clad in overalls, was before them, peering through thick rimless glasses that magnified his eyes in a peculiar way.

"Yeah? What is it?" When he spoke they found his deep-set eyes were matched by a voice that seemed to well from an endless cavern. Years had scarred his face with deep lines, and rheumatism had gnarled and twisted his body. He flailed his cane in the air.

Marcy watched, petrified, as her father extended his hand. "I'm Tom Dunlap and this is my family. We're the new tenants."

The old man scowled at Marcy and Phil. His thin lips made a straight line that was almost like another crease in his wrinkled face. "Ain't s'posed to be no younguns."

Marcy's father was a tall, thin man whose closely-clipped hair made him look even taller. His relaxed, easy-going manner was always a comfort to his family, but now as he spoke Marcy could tell that he was annoyed.

"They're not children. They're almost eleven and twelve. They won't disturb anyone."

Phil stood tall. He was growing so fast that he seemed all lanky arms and legs, and he resented being called a "youngun." Anyway, since he'd seen the ravine he just had to stay here.

Marcy's gaze moved from her father to Phil, then to her mother and back to the scowling old man. She tried to put on her angelic expression, though it was difficult for such a tomboy.

The old man growled, "Nobody but grownups is allowed in these apartments." With a hand crippled by arthritis he pushed his heavy glasses up on his bulbous nose.

"But didn't the realtor tell you?" Mr. Dunlap went on. "He knew about Marcy and Phil. I've already signed a lease for the summer."

"I keep telling them this ain't no place for younguns," the old man persisted. His scowl, the peering eyes, the large nose—all topped by wild grey hair—frightened Marcy.

At last Mrs. Dunlap spoke, "Oh, if you mean on account of the ravine, don't worry. They won't get hurt."

Mr. Dunlap's patience had obviously been tried. "We've had a long trip down from New York. We're tired and eager to get settled. If you'll just show us—"

"There's no trespassing signs all over this place," the old

man interrupted in his harsh voice. Evidently he was referring to the old part of the inn that Marcy had seen. While they were talking, he had not moved from his original position before the door. Now and then he lifted his cane and let it fall to his side again.

"All right, Mr.—" her father began in a defeated manner.

"Crowe." The old man spat out his name. "Silas Crowe."

"All right, Mr. Crowe, at least let us stay overnight, and I'll speak to Mr. Beard at the realtor's office in the morning and get this straightened out."

Reluctantly the old fellow lifted the keys attached to his belt by a grimy string. Peering through his thick glasses, he rattled the keys until he'd singled out a certain one. With a shuffling step, as if his bowed legs were stiff, he moved to one of the massive doors on the left and again with much rattling of keys unlocked it.

Mrs. Dunlap caught her breath when the door was opened. "Why, it's beautiful!" she said.

The sitting room was ornately done with heavily-draped windows. Overstuffed furniture was arranged around a marble fireplace with a great mirror much like the one in the hall. Richly-designed furniture stood imposingly along papered walls.

Before Mrs. Dunlap could move to the kitchen, Silas Crowe was hobbling toward a narrow, dark stairwell. "This goes up to your bedroom and bathroom. More stairs take you to a second bedroom and bath." Again he frowned at the red-headed children and ran a hand across his mop of iron-grey hair.

"You mean this is a three-storied apartment?" their father asked.

"That's right. They cut it up that way when they

9

remodeled." His words came out as if he resented having to speak at all.

"If you want me," he mumbled, "knock loud on that door I came out of."

"Thank you," replied Mr. Dunlap. He was obviously annoyed over the turn things had taken.

The old man shuffled toward the door, muttering, "No place for younguns," under his breath. The moment his back was turned Phil dashed up the stairs that circled to the first bedroom. In an instant Marcy was behind him.

"Holy Mackerel!" he shouted from somewhere above her.

Following his voice, Marcy climbed more spiral stairs to a spacious bedroom with a slanted ceiling on one side. Her mouth stood open in awe until she shrieked, "This is our room!"

"You mean if that eccentric old man lets us stay." Phil liked to use big words and besides, he was trying not to be childish. He crossed to the window. "Say, we've got a good view of the ravine from here," he said.

Marcy's attention had been captured by an antique pitcher and washbasin that fit into a stand that had been made for them. There was an oval mirror on top like one she'd seen in a Western movie. The twin beds had brass bedposts. They just couldn't take everything in.

About that time their mother's voice came up as if from the bottom of a barrel. "Philip! Marcy! Come down and help bring our bags in."

Excitedly they raced down the two flights of spiral stairs. This might not be such a dull summer after all.

3.
Getting Acquainted

Now that Mr. Crowe was out of sight and the luggage was all in, Marcy and Phil just couldn't wait to explore. The minute Mrs. Dunlap gave them the go-ahead they dashed outside.

"Are you going down in it?" Marcy questioned, running after her brother. They found it incredible that just a few feet behind the bamboo hedge the steep precipice fell away into a gorge that stretched to the left and right as far as they could see.

"Say," said Phil, studying the situation, "that railroad track at the bottom isn't used anymore. Look, weeds have even grown over the rails."

It made Marcy dizzy to look over the edge where small trees and vines hugged the cliff and fanned out in a dense undergrowth.

"Are you going down?" she repeated.

Phil was thinking so seriously he didn't bother to answer. Instead, his slender legs carried him swiftly toward the bridge, a shock of red hair swinging.

"That *would* be the best place to climb down," thought Marcy. There they could hold on to the supports beneath the bridge.

While Marcy and Phil were still running around the edge of the ravine like monkeys in a cage, Mr. Dunlap came outside. Joining them, he marveled at the great wisteria vines that wound in Tarzan fashion around the tall pines, oaks, dogwoods and Carolina cherry trees. "Ah—" he breathed. stretching out his arms, "smell that sweet honeysuckle."

"Where's the honeysuckle?" asked Marcy, not wanting to miss a thing.

"Everywhere," her father answered. "See, there and there. The vine with the funnel-shaped yellow blooms on it."

The three of them walked out onto the old wooden bridge that covered the ravine. From the middle they had a good view of the front and one side of the inn. The front had been freshly painted and redecorated, but the sprawling side and rear were suffering from neglect. Many seasons had eaten into the wood, warped the boards, and peeled the paint. Panes had been broken in some of the windows, and shutters hung loose. Large-leafed vines ran rampant, even covering some of the windows. It looked for all the world like a haunted house.

"Why, that place has more gables than Nathaniel Hawthorne's *House of Seven Gables*!" exclaimed Phil.

Not wanting to admit she hadn't read the book Phil referred to, Marcy counted hurriedly. "Yes, it's got nine." At least she knew what a gable was.

Across the bridge the road opened into a lovely boulevard

bordered by mysterious-looking forests. The varying shades of green made it almost as colorful as the woods in autumn. The trees were fresh and bright, not tired-looking like some that suffered in the languid summer. Again their father pointed out the honeysuckle and the yellow jessamine running below and climbing into the trees.

"This is South Carolina's state flower," he said of the jessamine. "The tiny yellow trumpets give it the sweet smell, but they're deadly poisonous."

Something stirred in the underbrush and the scutter of a grey squirrel caught their attention. He sat up, watched them nervously with his shoe-button eyes, and scampered up a tall pine. They all laughed. It was a beautiful walk. Almost every step revealed some unexpected pleasure.

Following the winding road, they came to a small brick building with a heavy oak door.

"What do you know!" Mr. Dunlap exclaimed when he discovered it was the library. "How lucky can a man be!"

"But," said Phil, "if nasty old Mr. Crowe makes us get out, you may not be near the library after all."

"Don't worry about that, son. I'm sure Mr. Beard will take care of it in the morning."

Marcy wasn't worried. She beamed. Her daddy could fix just about anything.

They found that a Presbyterian church was next door to the library. And from there they had a view of the main street of the small town. There was little life to be seen, only an occasional car passing in these after-business hours. It all seemed so different from what they were accustomed to.

Crossing the wide street, they admired a fountain encircled with spreading juniper amid a riot of orange, red and yellow day lilies.

13

"Mother'll like that," Marcy smiled.

The imposing post office, with its long steps and shiny brass rails. sat catercornered on the other side of the street. Everything was spread out and roomy here. Woods, mostly tall pines reaching high to get their share of sunlight, began on the other side of the boulevard. Several dirt roads with signs reading "Private" in neat black letters led to almost secluded homes.

Coming back over the bridge they could see the great hulking machinery standing idle after a day's work on the new apartment building. Silhouetted against the lemon-colored sunset, the machines looked like prehistoric monsters rising on the horizon.

"Gee!" said Phil, "That bulldozer looks like a dinosaur." Laughingly the others agreed.

"Let's see if Mother has things lined up so she can come out too," their father said as they neared the inn. About that time they noticed Mrs. Dunlap had already come outside. She was standing on the veranda, smiling and talking to a handsome young couple.

"Tom! Children!" she called. "Come meet the Fergusons, our new neighbors across the hall."

After everyone had said hello, Marcy could tell that Phil was as itchy as she was to get back to the ravine. But just at that moment the mention of Mr. Crowe's name caught their attention. Already Marcy realized she was scared to death of that man.

"Mrs. Dunlap was just telling us of Mr. Crowe's greeting," young Ferguson grinned.

"Oh, yes," nodded Mr. Dunlap.

"It seems," said Ferguson's pretty wife, "that Mr. Crowe's parents were personal servants of the original

14

owners of this inn, and for some reason he acts as if he owns the place. I'm told he brought Mrs. Crowe here to live after they were married, and many years later when the inn closed she and Mr. Crowe stayed on as caretakers."

Then he does have a wife?" asked Mrs. Dunlap.

"Rumor has it that she went to Philadelphia five or six years ago, to live with relatives on her mother's side of the family," Ferguson said.

"I wouldn't blame her " said Mrs. Ferguson, with a glance toward her husband.

"He's eccentric," Phil put in.

They all smiled.

"That's for sure," agreed Ferguson. "Why, in the spring he even refused to allow a razing crew to tear down the dilapidated part of this building, after the new owners had given them instructions to do so."

"He went out with his cane and stopped them right in the act," Mrs. Ferguson added.

"And they let him?" asked Mr. Dunlap.

"He told them he had been given permission to live here the rest of his life," Ferguson said. "He lives in the old part, you know. Actually, I think they just pacified him by postponing it. The current owner definitely isn't going to renovate any more of this building with those new apartments coming up across the street."

"And the old section surely is an eyesore," said Mr. Dunlap.

"That it is," agreed Ferguson.

Phil didn't think it was an eyesore, and neither did Marcy. They liked the way it looked. As quickly as the conversation switched to the Dunlaps' reason for coming south, Phil rounded the corner of the inn with Marcy following close behind.

15

Standing next to the hedge that bordered their side of the ravine, Phil studied the old building.

"Look! That's our room—way up there."

"Which one?"

"The gabled window with the fire escape by it and the one to the right of it."

"I'm gonna have the bed by the fire escape," Marcy said, and looked at Phil for an argument.

But Phil had no time to argue. He had already run back to the bridge. If she knew her brother, he was figuring the best way to get to the bottom of that ravine.

4.

A Discovery

Their parents had called them in before they'd had time to get to the bottom of the ravine, but they'd explored enough for Marcy to know it would be no easy task. Phil would find a way. She knew that.

As Marcy lay in her bed by the fire escape window, she thought of the fun she'd had already. Even taking a bath was nice here, in the quaint old bathtub with its claw feet.

"Phil?" Marcy called across to her brother's bed. "Why do you think Mr. Crowe doesn't want us here?"

"Because he's odd. Dad says we'll stay and we will."

Marcy turned on her stomach and bunched her pillow under her chin. Her long auburn hair fell around her shoulders. "Phil, have you ever been down a fire escape?"

"Just think—*I* have to room with Miss Chatterbox for a whole summer."

Ignoring her brother's remark, Marcy said, "But in case

17

there's a fire, shouldn't we know how to go down the fire escape?"

"What do you suggest? A fire drill—now?" Phil mocked her.

"Oh, no, not now," Marcy answered quickly, peering around her bedpost and out into the night.

"Then keep quiet and go to sleep," he ordered.

But Marcy wasn't in the mood for sleep. Her mind was crowded with thoughts about the old inn. She thought of all the famous people who must have slept here in its days of splendor, and of the gay balls they must have had. Then she lay listening to the night sounds: the breathing of the wind, the faint tapping of a loose shutter, the chirping of crickets. Somewhere across the ravine a sweet-throated bird was singing. At first it sounded like the mew of a cat, then more like the whistle of a train. Noises kept sifting in from outside. An occasional car crossed over the bridge.

Marcy always thought of this as the "whisper time" of night. How different it was here from the whisper time in New York. She looked up into the velvet darkness of the sky. Summer stars twinkled at her, but she found no warmth in them. Suddenly the strangeness of it all chilled her. "Why," she wondered, "doesn't Mr. Crowe want us here?"

"Phil?" she called in a low voice.

The steady breathing from the other bed told her Phil was fast asleep.

Marcy had always prided herself on not being a fraidy-cat, and she wasn't afraid now, she told herself. All of a sudden she remembered Herman, the stuffed frog she always carried with her for luck. He was still in her suitcase.

Slipping her feet to the floor, Marcy crossed the room in the faint moonlight. Bending over, she rummaged among the contents of her suitcase until she felt the familiar body. Instinctively she hugged the animal to her and was just straightening up when she collided with someone.

Her mother gasped, "Oh, Marcy! You startled me."

"Me too," Marcy said in embarrassment.

"I just wanted to check on you," her mother whispered, realizing now that Phil was asleep. "You seem so far away."

"I'm okay. I'll knock on the floor and yell if I need you," Marcy whispered, laughing.

"All right." Mrs. Dunlap gave her daughter a squeeze and tiptoed back downstairs.

Her mother's visit and Herman's closeness returned Marcy's confidence. Instead of getting back into bed, she stood by her window. It was open. She pressed her nose against the screen in order to see down the far end of the ravine. The moonlight lay on the rails in long streaks of silver.

Suddenly, without warning, the screen slipped from the window and fell to rest on the fire escape. At first Marcy was alarmed but then, realizing what had happened, she eased herself up into the window and strained to make out shadowy shapes in the darkness.

"This is like the balcony in the movies," she thought. Across the ravine she could see the outline of trees, black against the night sky. In the dim shadows along the woods, fireflies scattered stardust as they played hide and seek in the edge of darkness. The moon hung above the trees like a great bubble. A cloud floated over it. Marcy's eyes burned from staring into the thick night and she squeezed them tight.

When she opened her eyes again and looked down into the narrow ravine, she caught her breath. Two figures were walking along the railroad track, going away from the inn. She could see them silhouetted against the night. Marcy

19

couldn't quite make out the dim forms, but one of them looked like the hulking body of Mr. Crowe. Whoever it was, he was holding onto someone else, and they were moving slowly, very slowly, up the track.

Now how had they gotten into the ravine? And why would they be walking up the track at this time of night?

Suddenly the night air was colder than Marcy had thought. Shakily she climbed through the window, reached for the screen, and fit it back into place. She pulled down her window and locked it. Climbing into bed she pulled up her coverlet and hugged Herman to her. This was going to be quite a summer. Already there were so many questions with no answers. She wished Phil were awake so she could tell him what she'd seen.

"Phil?" she whispered again. Only his rhythmic breathing answered her.

5.
A Mysterious Happening

When Marcy woke up the next morning, for a bewildered moment she couldn't remember where she was. Then the events of yesterday came rushing back. She sat up in bed and looked out her window. The day was beautiful and sunny. Envious that Phil was already up, she threw on her clothes, ran a brush through her long hair and hurried downstairs.

Mr. Dunlap was in his usual good mood at breakfast and was eager to get started on his research. Besides that, he'd never found such a wonderful climate. Last night had been perfect for sleeping.

"I'll dash by Mr. Beard's office and confirm our lease, then go on to the library. Will you meet me there later?" Mr. Dunlap looked at his wife and children.

"I'd love to," Mrs. Dunlap said, "I have very little unpacking left to do, but I do have to find a grocery store before lunch."

"Phil? Marcy?" their father asked.

Marcy looked at Phil. She didn't want to go, and she knew wild horses couldn't drag Phil away this morning.

"Maybe this afternoon, Dad," Phil said. "I'd like to look around here this morning."

"Me too," added Marcy.

"All right, but do be careful around that ravine," Mr. Dunlap said.

"And by all means," put in their mother, "stay away from the construction across the street."

"And Mr. Crowe," thought Marcy.

As Phil and Marcy helped clear the breakfast dishes, Mrs. Dunlap reminded them repeatedly how grown up and responsible they were now.

"If anything happens while we're away," she cautioned, "one of you just run up to the library. Daddy tells me it's just across the bridge."

* * *

No sooner had their mother headed for the library than Marcy and Phil ran to the ravine. The noise from the construction site was going full blast now, and they had to shout above it to hear each other.

They found the bridge was not a good place to go down after all. The wooden supports were splintery, and it would be impossible to slide down with summer shorts on. Phil quickly spied a spot that was less dense in undergrowth, and turning around backwards he started down.

"If these scrub oaks will hold me," he called up to Marcy, "they're bound to hold you. Come on."

Marcy was game. With a slight quickening in her stomach, she turned around and dropped her body over the edge. For a moment she was suspended until her foot searched for and found a hold.

Painstakingly she inched downward, feeling along the steep incline for one firm foothold after another. Once she slipped and lost her footing, and several times her hair caught in twigs. Afraid to turn loose to free it she went on down, leaving strands of hair behind.

"How much farther?" she called, not daring to look below.

"I'm almost there!" Phil shouted. And then a resounding bump told her he'd reached the bottom.

If Phil could, she could. With renewed vigor Marcy felt below her and again shifted her weight. Half sliding and half climbing, she worked her way down the steep embankment.

At last, hot and scratchy, she made it. There were red marks on her legs and arms and her hands stung from holding onto the branches so tightly. Perspiration made little rivulets down her face.

Marcy pushed her hair back and looked up at the sky. "Whew!" she said. They were going to have to get out of this place, but she wouldn't think about that now.

Phil was down on his hands and knees with his head to the rail. Marcy couldn't imagine why, but she did the same. The cold steel of the rail felt good to her stinging hands. The tarry smell of the crossties permeated the air.

"I read," said Phil, lifting his head, "that you can hear a train coming miles and miles away like that."

Marcy jumped up. "But you said this track wasn't used anymore." The idea of a train coming now wasn't a pleasant one. There were just a few feet on either side of the track.

"It isn't. I was just telling you what I've read." Phil turned toward the bridge and started walking a rail, balancing himself by holding his hands out on either side of his body.

Marcy copied him. "Gee, this is fun!" she called. The sound of the workers from above was faint down in the gorge, and their voices had an odd, hollow sound as they called to each other.

Slipping and laughing and getting up again, they walked the rails side by side until they had crossed under the bridge. Still for as far as they could see the great cut in the earth went on.

"We'd better turn around," Marcy said.

"I guess so," Phil agreed, "but we can't get lost. All we'd have to do is just follow the track."

They turned and started back toward the inn, still tottering and giggling in their attempts to walk the rails without slipping onto the loose gravel between the crossties.

"Hey, see if you can do it with your eyes closed!" called Phil. He had mastered his first attempts to balance himself on the slender rail, and now he wanted more of a challenge.

They were almost under the bridge again when Marcy nearly slipped. She opened her eyes and looked up. For a moment she stood stock-still, too frightened to move or call out. Mr. Crowe was coming down the railroad track toward them!

"Ph-Phil—"

"Huh?"

"Look!" She pointed to the hunched figure with his head down, picking his way along with his cane.

Immediately Phil darted behind the base of the bridge. "Come on. We can hide here until he passes," he whispered.

"But he'll see us." Marcy's voice sounded strange and unfamiliar to her.

"Not if we hide behind these bushes."

"But—"

"But what?" Phil was getting impatient.

Marcy didn't want to admit it, but she remembered seeing

lizards scurry around wooded areas. Not that she'd mind holding one, but she didn't want one slithering up her leg uninvited.

"Come on!" Phil urged.

Mustering courage, she squeezed into the place Phil provided. After all, a lizard was the lesser of the two evils.

They hid behind the great wooden beams for what seemed like an eternity to Marcy before Phil whispered, "I'm going to peek out."

Frightened, Marcy watched as the look on his face changed to one of consternation.

"Where'd he go?" he said half aloud.

"He's gone?" Marcy asked.

"He sure is," said Phil, coming out of hiding. He stood there scratching his head and studying the embankment on either side.

"He couldn't have climbed up," he said.

"Heavens, no," Marcy said, coming out from behind the bridge. She almost relaxed enough to giggle at the thought of that old man climbing the ravine.

"Come on, let's look down this way."

"Phil, I think we'd better get out of here."

"Don't worry, we will—just as soon as I find out how old Mr. Crowe got out."

Halfheartedly Marcy followed her brother down the tracks. He was walking on the crossties and moving so rapidly he skipped one now and then. Marcy had to run to keep up with him. All the while he was examining the side of the ravine that was below the inn.

"Philip!" Marcy gasped.

"What?" Phil whirled around to face his sister.

"I forgot to tell you—last night after you went to sleep—I

26

looked out of my window and saw two people walking in the ravine—down that way," she pointed ahead.

"Then there *has* to be an exit somewhere."

They moved on farther, slowing down now and then to examine the wall of the gorge. As far as they could see it was covered with small vines and bushes. A different kind of broad-leaf vine ran over the other growth and in places even hid the earth.

"Look, Phil, there's a path," Marcy said in a hushed voice.

"Good work," whispered Phil, following its route with his eyes. The praise from her brother boosted Marcy's morale and she looked with him.

At the same moment their searching eyes fell upon a door, almost hidden by hanging vines. At one time it had been painted green; now, weather-worn, it blended with the background so that it was hardly noticeable.

"It must be locked from the inside now," whispered Phil.

"Don't try it!" begged Marcy. "Let's go. Please, Phil." If Mr. Crowe appeared at that door, she'd die in her tracks. Her knees felt weak. If they waited much longer, she'd never make it up that embankment.

Phil stepped back and looked up at the earth between the door and the old inn. "That means this house has rooms below ground level," he mused.

"I'm going, Phil," Marcy started to retreat. The thought of Mr. Crowe coming out of that door chilled her bones. She squinched her eyes as Phil tried the handle.

"Okay, I'm coming, but I'm not forgetting that door. That's for sure."

Phil found the place where they'd come down, and they started the ascent. Much to Marcy's surprise, pulling herself up wasn't nearly so difficult as the trip down.

She stayed close behind Phil and when they reached the top and started inside the inn, Marcy asked, "Are you going to tell Mom and Dad about the door?"

"Not yet, and don't you tell them. This means we'll have to explore from the inside, and they may not let us do that."

For a second Marcy was peeved that Phil had implied she couldn't keep secrets, and then his last words pushed that thought from her mind. *Explore from the inside*, he'd said. Marcy's heart skipped a beat.

6.
The Library

Marcy and Phil didn't have to worry at the moment about not mentioning the door in the ravine to their parents. Mr. Dunlap came in at noon excited over the marvelous collection of old newspapers at the library, and Mrs. Dunlap had found the librarian, Miss Pettus, to be one of the most delightful persons she had ever met.

"And just think, Tom," their mother said, "they'd been looking everywhere for a substitute librarian for the summer."

"You're going to do it then?" he asked enthusiastically.

Her brown eyes twinkled. She shared her husband's love for books. "I'd love to, if there are no objections. It's close to the apartment, and the children love to read."

"What about it—Marcy? Phil?" Mr. Dunlap asked.

Marcy opened her mouth to speak, then hesitated and looked at Phil. Taking the cue he said, "It's okay by me."

Phil knew he mustn't appear too enthusiastic over his mother's working. Mrs. Dunlap was smart; she might suspect they'd need her away to carry out his plans.

"Yes, Mom, Phil and I will be okay." Marcy added. "We'll read and—and—gee, that ravine is cool." She looked at Phil to see if she'd said too much.

"I noticed your shoes were all smudged from the railroad," their mother said, but then she smiled.

"We've been walking the rails," Phil said quickly.

"And did you know, my offsprings," Mr. Dunlap used his most theatrical manner, "that you were walking right on history itself?"

"Really?" they both asked.

"Really. That railroad was the first one to carry passengers in America. It ran from Charleston, South Carolina, to a little town on the Savannah River called Hamburg—a town with one of the most fascinating histories you've ever heard."

"Do you mean that's the track the Best Friend ran on?" Phil asked. "I studied that in social studies."

"That's right," his father said. "Of course, the original track wasn't in that exact spot—it was through the center of town, but the train was unable to pull up Aiken's hill, so this gorge had to be cut."

Like his father, Phil had a real interest in history. "That track was pretty long for those days, wasn't it, Dad?"

"Yes—136 miles, to be exact. If you'll go back to the library with us, I'll show you some material on it. You know, the Best Friend had a short lifetime. It seems a Negro fireman became annoyed by the noise of the escaping steam and sat on the safety valve. He was killed instantly and the Best Friend was almost completely destroyed."

"How terrible!" said Mrs. Dunlap.

30

"Yes, it was," her husband agreed. "It was rebuilt, but then they named it the Phoenix." Nothing delighted their father more than sharing his knowledge of history, and he always had an enthusiastic audience in his family.

"How fast do you think it went?" asked Phil.

"Oh, fifteen to twenty-five miles an hour, and they thought that was really traveling." Mr. Dunlap smiled. "The passengers rode in open coaches, and the smoke from the stack left them smudged and blackened with soot and ashes."

"Oh, Tom," said Mrs. Dunlap, "Miss Pettus said legend has it that a romance caused the railroad to be laid through Aiken rather than some other place."

"Oh, you women are such romantics," her husband laughed.

"Really!" Mrs. Dunlap was excited now, and Marcy and Phil listened attentively, momentarily forgetting about Mr. Crowe and the ravine. "She said you may not find it recorded, but it was rumored that the girl's father wouldn't approve marriage unless one of the regular scheduled stops would be his plantation near here."

"And what does rumor say this young suitor's name was?" her husband teased.

"Dexter, Alfred A. Dexter, a young civil engineer from Boston."

"Why, he's the one who laid out the city of Aiken," Mr. Dunlap said. "He planned these 200-foot-wide streets and centered them with parkways."

"Maybe that's why he laid out the city with such painstaking care," Mrs. Dunlap defended her rumor. "Maybe he was stalling for more time to be near his sweetheart."

"Maybe, but I rather think this Dexter was a man who with much foresight and wisdom, not romance, laid out the

31

geometric plan for this lovely town."

"Then why wasn't the town named for him?" asked Phil.

"Because it was named for the man who made the railroad possible, an Irishman who came to America when he was eight years old—William Aiken. He was the leader of those who wanted the railroad built and was first president of the Carolina Railroad and Canal Company."

"Oh, dear, it's almost two o'clock," said Mrs. Dunlap, jumping up from the table.

Suddenly the frightening experience of the morning ran through Marcy's mind, and she thought of what Phil had said about going inside the old inn. A shiver ran down her spine.

Her mother noticed. "Marcy, don't you feel well? You're not having a chill?"

Before she could answer her father said, "They probably played too hard this morning. A trip to the library should calm them down a bit."

"Yeah," said Phil. "A trip to the library will cure almost anything, won't it. Dad?"

* * *

A trip to the library it was. Not that Phil and Marcy didn't enjoy libraries—they'd been brought up on them—but just now something else was monopolizing their attention. For the time being, however, that would have to wait.

On their way to the library Phil remembered to ask his father about his trip to the realtor's office.

"Oh, he said to ignore the poor old fellow," his father answered. "You were right, Phil. He is eccentric."

"You know," said Mrs. Dunlap as she walked briskly beside her husband, "Miss Pettus said for years the towns-people tried to be nice to the Crowes. Especially after the inn

32

closed, but they were just plain standoffish, or he was. No one seems to know very much about his wife, except that her mother was "society" from Philadelphia and married a Southern gentleman. And Mrs. Crowe's family, it seems, disowned her when she married her riding instructor."

Marcy's face registered disbelief. "You mean Mr. Crowe was a riding instructor?" She just couldn't think of him as anything but a crotchety, crabby old man.

"Well, whatever he was," said her father, "I can't understand how anyone can live with himself and be so ill-tempered."

Marcy looked at her father, who didn't have a crabby bone in his body, and grinned.

"Neither can I," said Mrs. Dunlap, "but Miss Pettus said for the last five or six years he's lived almost like a hermit."

The woods on their right were teeming with the scurry of little inhabitants. Birds fluttered from branch to branch, twittering and chirping. Marcy thought how nice it would be to sit in the coolness of the woods and daydream. Another time she would, she promised herself.

They could see the library now, and an enormous shaggy dog sitting outside the door. Evidently he was waiting for his master who was inside. As they came nearer, Marcy saw that he looked friendly. She reached out and patted his head. He licked her hand and wagged his tail.

When they entered the library, a wiry little woman ran from behind a shiny oval desk and came to greet them. Marcy thought she looked terribly thin, with hollows and shadows in her face—almost as if she didn't get enough to eat. A little silver chain attached to her eyeglasses hung around a neck that was as thin and gaunt as that of a baby bird stretching for food.

33

"This must be Marcia and Philip," she beamed, holding out a bony hand to each of them.

"Yes," their mother smiled, "and this is Miss Pettus." The minute Marcy heard Miss Pettus speak she knew what her mother meant when she said Miss Pettus was delightful. Her eyes lit up when she spoke and her voice filled with wonder, as if she were telling a deep, dark secret. Marcy liked her immediately, even if she did need fattening up.

"Mr. Dunlap," the librarian said, with a note of awe in her soft voice, "your nook is waiting for you, and I've put you some new material there."

"Great!" he said. Making a circle in the air with his thumb and forefinger, he headed for the stacks.

Mrs. Dunlap went behind the desk as Miss Pettus ushered Phil and Marcy over to a table where a tanned, dark-haired boy was reading. "Jerry," she said, "I want you to meet Philip and Marcia Dunlap. They are here for the summer and are living at the old Telfair Inn."

Marcy thought she saw Jerry stiffen when Miss Pettus mentioned the inn.

The librarian went on in her small, fascinating voice, "Jerry's sister is about your age, Marcy. She's at camp this week, but I'm sure you'll enjoy each other when she gets back. Make yourselves at home now." She turned back to her duties. A mother with two small children had come into the library and she went over to them and began talking in her exciting way again.

Noticing Jerry's book, Phil spoke, "*Waterless Mountain—* I've read that. It's good." He and Marcy sat down at the table.

Marking his place, Jerry closed the book, squirmed in his chair, and spoke in a soft drawl, "It's okay. I don't like to read too much, but I'm in the summer reading club, and this is on the list." Then his face brightened. "The teacher'll give you an extra *A* next year if you join the club."

Marcy was about to get up to look for a book when Jerry asked, "Do you really live at the inn?"

"Since yesterday," said Phil.

"Have you seen old man Crowe?"

Marcy opened her mouth to speak, but Phil beat her to the draw, "Yeah, we've seen him." His look told Marcy to keep still.

"Scarey old man, isn't he?" Jerry said with a frown.

"Yeah, he didn't want us to live there," Phil told him.

"He doesn't like kids. You know that cane he carries?"

"Yeah."

"He doesn't really need it. He just has it to chase kids with."

Gooseflesh rippled over Marcy's arms. Momentarily she relived the episode of yesterday when Mr. Crowe was headed down the ravine toward them.

"Some people say that old inn's haunted," Jerry went on.

Phil figured he'd better stop this conversation before Jerry learned of his plans. Glancing at Marcy, he could tell she was dying to find out if Jerry knew about the door in the ravine wall, but Phil thought it better not to tell a soul. Not yet. He got up and said, "There sure are a lot of birds in this town."

"Yeah, it's against the law to shoot one," Jerry said. Somehow Marcy got the idea that if it weren't Jerry would enjoy shooting them.

"Is that your dog outside?" she asked.

Jerry nodded his head and grinned, "Follows me everywhere I go. He gives the teachers a fit when school's on."

The three of them smiled at each other.

35

"See you later," Phil said as he headed for the stacks. Marcy went over to her mother at the desk, and Jerry let out a long sigh and opened his book again.

They had fun in the library. Phil checked out a book on South Carolina birds, and Marcy got *Wind in the Chimney*. For the next few hours they read, browsed in the stacks, and listened while their father showed them pictures and told them more local history.

Like her parents, Marcy loved a library. She liked its smell, a kind of mixture of old leather, paste, newsprint, and oiliness of the floor—all were comforting and familiar odors to her. She felt a kinship here.

The afternoon passed quickly and soon they were headed back to the inn, each with books for the oncoming night.

As Marcy helped her mother prepare hamburgers for dinner, they talked of the events of the afternoon. That evening Marcy sat at the tall mahogany secretary and wrote Ellen a long, long letter.

7.
Trespassing

When Marcy awoke the next morning to find yellow sunlight streaking across her floor, she knew she'd slept later than usual. She hadn't meant to. Today promised too much excitement to sleep.

Hurriedly she slipped on an old pair of cut-off jeans she'd raveled and a striped T-shirt, gave her hair a hasty brushing before catching it up in a rubber band, and ran downstairs. Even though she was still shivery over the prospect of going inside the inn, her curiosity outweighed her fears.

When she bounced down the stairs, her parents were still at the breakfast table, drinking a second cup of coffee and reading the paper. Marcy fixed herself a bowl of cereal and ate it so quickly it didn't have time to get soggy in the milk. Then as quick as a flash she dashed outside to join Phil.

Within minutes after their parents left for the library, Marcy and Phil were stepping cautiously over uneven grey stones to the other side of the inn, a part they hadn't yet observed. The short boulevard on this side looked deserted.

"Are we really going inside?" Marcy asked.

"Of course."

"But, Phil, it does say no trespassing. There's the sign." Marcy pointed to a weatherworn board nailed to a black-trunked magnolia that bordered the street. Scrawled in crude printing was *NO TRESSPASSING!*

The truth of the matter was that Jerry's words, "Some people say that old inn is haunted," still rang in Marcy's ears.

Vines tangled in broken windows and old bricks and boards were heaped in piles. Phil moved closer to the building and began edging himself between boards that had been torn loose. He was losing no time.

"Come on." He waved his arm to motion Marcy on. For a moment she hesitated.

"If you're chicken," he taunted, "you don't have to come."

Just enough of Marcy's temper flared to give her courage. "I'm not chicken," she retorted. "It's just that Mom and Dad wouldn't like it one little bit if they knew." Getting no answer from her brother, she took a deep breath and inched her way into the opening after him.

"This must be where the razing crew started," whispered Phil over his shoulder.

Thankful that their rubber-soled sneakers made little noise, they stepped carefully into an enormous room. Obviously this had been the original front entrance, for there was a desk like one in a hotel, with dust-covered mailboxes behind it. Signs of desolation and decay lay over the deserted room. Cobwebs hung from the ceiling. Stealthily they crept on into an adjoining room where many-paned windows lined one

whole wall. Shreds of rotted draperies sagged from French windows that were broken and dirty. Through the windows they caught glimpses of a stone terrace half covered by the broad-leaf vine.

"This must have been the dining room," whispered Marcy.

Stepping cautiously on the treacherously rotted floor, they made their way around fallen wainscoting into another room as large as the dining room. Dirt daubers' nests in long chunks of mud plastered the corners. A huge fireplace with fire-blackened stones added an ashy smell to the dusty room. Above the fireplace, a mantel shelf held the dust of all the years since a fire had been lit on the hearth below. A spider crawled up the wall toward a big cobweb that draped itself from the high ceiling to a corner of the mantel. The creepy-crawly sensation that had come over Marcy when she first entered the inn intensified itself.

As Marcy and Phil lifted their feet over the tangle of splintered lumber and broken plaster that lay in heaps on the floor, Marcy imagined the rooms had once been furnished as lavishly as their apartment. In a way it was sad to see these rooms that used to be bright and gay now empty and run-down.

Picking his way, Phil entered a hallway to another wing of the old building. Marcy followed him like a shadow. The big house ticked with silence. In spite of their soft shoes, their footsteps caused the house to creak and groan. It was darker now in the corridor, and there were dust motes dancing in the light that filtered in from other rooms. There were doors and more doors leading off the hallway. Most of them were closed.

Marcy held her breath as Phil tried one. It creaked in complaint, moved, and swung slowly open. This room, too, was empty and suffering from neglect.

"There must be two hundred rooms in this inn," whispered Phil.

They tried to move surreptiously like Indians until they reached the end of the hallway, where there was a winding staircase like the one in their apartment.

"Maybe this leads to the basement," said Phil.

Marcy opened her mouth, but no words came out. After several tries, she found her voice. "O-Oh, Phil, you're not—going down there!"

"Why not?"

Marcy's throat tightened in fear. Surely her blood had stopped running in her veins! Was Phil as brave as he tried to sound? She'd never been more frightened in her whole life. The air was close and musty around them as they descended the steep, dimly-lit staircase.

All of a sudden Phil came to a halt. He could go no further. The stairwell had been boarded up. He darted around Marcy and back up the steps to the landing. In his haste he stubbed his toe. Looking down, he saw where more boards had been nailed—this time across the floor.

Marcy rushed to Phil's side and watched shakily while he knelt down and got a firm grip on one of the larger planks. He yanked and the heap of rubble seemed to fall apart. Boards and timber crashed. A cloud of dust spiraled. Marcy had shut her eyes against the impact. When she opened them, Phil had disappeared!

"Phil? Phil? Where are you?" She heard her voice call louder than she meant it to as she frantically waved at the dust that had surrounded her.

Like a voice rolling up from a dark pit, he answered, "I'm down here."

"In that hole, for goodness sake?"

"Yeah, I think it must have been an old elevator shaft." His voice echoed and re-echoed in the narrow hole.

"Are you hurt?"

"N-No, I don't think so. Somehow I caught onto some old ropes."

"What'll we do now?" Phil had really gone too far this time, and Marcy felt herself on the verge of tears.

"I see an opening of light. You come down."

"Come down! How can I?"

"Like you did in the ravine. Turn around backwards and let your feet follow the ropes hanging on the sides. Come on. I'll guide you."

Knowing they'd gone too far to turn back, Marcy took a shaky breath and turned around to let herself down. Her legs shook with tension. Even the muscles around her mouth and eyes felt tight. As she clung for dear life, the rope swung slightly, bumping her against the sides, but finally she made it.

Just as she reached the bottom, Phil clamped his hand hard over her mouth. Luckily she'd seen it coming or it would have scared the daylights out of her.

"S-s-s-s-s-h-h! Be still. Listen!" he said.

A definite sound came from the other side of the wall. They held their breath and listened. There was a low crooning like someone singing, and then all was quiet. Crouching against the wall, they strained their ears for a sound.

"Oh, please, Phil, let's go," begged Marcy. With a trembling hand she brushed the veil of spiderwebs from her hair. She didn't care any more if he said she was chicken. "I'm scared."

"Oh, all right," he said, and Marcy had the feeling Phil wasn't as brave as he pretended to be. He went on, "Let's see if we can find some stairs. We're below ground level."

Moving cautiously through the corridor, they came upon another staircase. Already flushed from the morning's escapade, they rushed upstairs and down another long hallway.

Marcy felt as if they had been moving in this maze of rooms and halls for hours. It was all more like a bad dream. She just couldn't believe it was happening. She'd always wanted to explore an old house, but she hadn't known it would be like this. As they zigzagged in an effort to find an exit, it was easy for Marcy to believe this spooky section of the inn did house ghosts, the kind that wore white sheets and clanked chains and moaned.

Finally, panting and puffing, they came to a door that led to the outside. With reckless haste Phil tried the handle but found it locked. White and breathless, Marcy trailed him through more dust and cobwebs until he said, "Here, we can climb out this window."

Crawling through the vine-covered window, they found themselves on an aged stone terrace. As quickly as they could get their bearings, they broke into a run toward the entrance to their apartment. Once Marcy stumbled and fell, but she was up again in an instant. They'd almost reached the corner when they heard an angry shout behind them. Looking over their shoulders, they saw Mr. Crowe waving his cane in the air and bellowing at them.

"Git along!" he roared with an impatient motion of his cane. Marcy panicked as Phil's strong legs kept him several paces ahead of her.

When at last they reached the corner and looked back, out of breath, old man Crowe was still standing there glaring. He lifted his cane in another furious gesture.

"What a crab!" Phil panted as they flung themselves on the steps of the veranda.

Marcy's heart pounded furiously. Her legs shook from running and her breath came in short jerks. She forced a breath of relief that almost turned to a sob. Tears flooded her eyes. Batting them away, she noticed Phil's freckled face had a sickly greenish cast beneath the dirt and dust he'd accumulated in his fall. She knew now that he was frightened too. But she knew another thing too—he'd never admit it, and if she dared so much as suggest that he was scared, he wouldn't like her for a whole week, maybe not forever. Marcy was glad she was a girl, at least right now. It was okay for a girl to be scared now and then.

"I don't like him, Phil."

"After this I don't either."

"He gives me the creeps. I think we'd better tell Mom and Dad."

"No, Marcy! Don't be a dope." Phil was stern. "They won't leave us alone any more if you tell."

"But what if he tells on us?"

"Don't worry. He won't. There's something down there he doesn't want us to know about, and if he tells, it'll make him look suspicious. He won't tell."

"I only hope you're right," Marcy said doubtfully. And as an afterthought she added, "But Phil, we may be in danger."

"As long as we stay out of the old man's way, we're not in danger. That's all we gotta do—stay out of Mr. Crowe's way."

8.
Wild Goose Chase

When Mr. Dunlap was engaged in research, he was always ready for what his family called a "wild goose chase." This meant that the family would pile into the car and go chasing over the countryside looking for markers or information, following up what he had found in old newspapers and letters. And always, as his family knew so well, his secret dream was to find something not yet recorded in history books.

Today was a perfect day for a "wild goose chase" as far as the rest of the family was concerned. Mrs. Dunlap had the day off from the library, and as for Marcy, she'd had enough earthshaking excitement to last for a long time. The hardest part of all was to keep quiet about it. Several times she actually had to bite her tongue or push it hard against her teeth to keep from telling about yesterday and their frightening experience. She was glad, too, to get away from the inn. She certainly didn't want to take the chance of running into Mr. Crowe any time soon!

Having acquired partial directions, Mr. Dunlap left Aiken by way of Pine Log Road and headed toward Augusta, Georgia.

"This road was a famous Tory trail to Fort Moore during the Revolutionary War," he told his family. "In fact, it was when that trail was being established that a huge pine fell across the South Edisto River, providing a natural bridge and giving the road its name of Pine Log."

"How fascinating!" said Mrs. Dunlap.

"Where are we going first, Dad?" asked Marcy.

"I thought we'd explore around a famous old dueling ground—Sand Bar Ferry, it's called."

"Great!" said Phil. "I read a book about dueling in England. They used swords."

"Even back then there were laws to prevent dueling, but these affairs were kept secret," said his father.

"You mean they had duels in this country?" asked Marcy, bouncing on the edge of her seat.

"Sit back, will you!" griped Phil. That was the thing about older brothers—they did like to be bossy.

The Dunlaps passed an area along the highway that was being newly developed with small homes. Most of the trees here were pines and water oaks.

"To answer your question, Marcy," her father said, "People who came to this country brought their customs with them. There were still those, especially among the aristocracy, who believed wounded honor could be healed only with blood. In this country, though, the weapons were nearly always pistols."

"I'm glad we don't settle grievances that way now," said

Mrs. Dunlap. "Think how much heartache and grief they must have caused."

"Why would a dueling ground be called a ferry?" asked Phil. He didn't like to see the sad expression on his mother's face and was eager to change the subject.

Well-researched as usual, his father was ready with the answers. "It was named for the ferry that crossed the Savannah River. You see, there was a level sand bar on the Georgia side that ran along the river and into the woods. The South Carolinians dueled there and then crossed the state line by ferry before the constables from Georgia could arrest them."

"Say, that was sneaky!" said Phil.

"The Georgians did the same," his father replied. "They dueled on the South Carolina side, on a high bluff where Fort Moore was situated in colonial days. Then their parties would recross by ferry to Georgia for the same reasons."

"Parties?" said Marcy in disbelief.

"That means the two principals engaged in the conflict, two seconds, a surgeon and sometimes a few friends."

"I still think it's gruesome," said Mrs. Dunlap. "It shouldn't have been permitted."

"You remember," said her husband, "I said it was a gentleman's way of settling an insult. A gentleman of the South is never a coward. Many people, especially Northerners, felt as you do about dueling. There were many harsh digs at the practice of dueling south of the Mason-Dixon line. But even the governor of South Carolina felt that if an individual were deeply wronged, he should deal with it in the language and manner of a gentleman. Even the challenge to a duel was written in the most formal manner."

"It's still astonishing that the leaders of a state would

47

condone such barbarism," insisted his wife.

Mr. Dunlap relished his family's enthusiasm for history. "Why in 1838 Governor Wilson of South Carolina compiled a code of honor for duelers to follow. According to his code, one man was never allowed to take unfair advantage of the other. No fight was ever to be continued after one man was wounded."

"Is the ferry still there?" asked Marcy, becoming a little impatient with the governor's code of honor.

"Probably not. Why, here we are," said Mr. Dunlap, pulling off the highway next to the Sand Bar Ferry Bridge.

As the four of them climbed from the car, they could see the muddy waters of the Savannah churning swiftly over great rocks, on its way to the Atlantic Ocean. They walked onto the Carolina side of the bridge, where they found a plaque. Mr. Dunlap read the legend of the bridge aloud as he recorded it in his little black book.

This bridge, erected upon the site
of the old Sand Bar Ferry,
stands as a memorial to a spot famous
in the history of Georgia and South Carolina.

The ferry served as a crossing place
and medium of communication between
the peoples of these two great states.

This spot has been the rendezvous for
settlements of affairs of honour,
which were the topics of toasts
of many tales told in vengeful mien,
or whispered in bated breath, while
hearts have ached and burst with grief.

The raging waters of the Savannah have
washed away the blood stains from the
sands which around are smiling through
the dew, where tears once trembled on

the grass. Progress, young and strong
has subdued these evils dark, and those
tragic scenes have passed into oblivion,
save for faint memory and old folk tales.

Satisfied that the river had changed its course since 1875,
the date of the last recorded duel at this famous battle-
ground, and that the Savannah River had truly "washed away
the blood stains from the sand," the Dunlaps crossed the
bridge into Georgia.

In the city of Augusta they located the Magnolia Cemetery, where they visited the tomb of the last known young
man to have been killed in a duel there.

Phil was first to see the grave, so he read the inscription,
"Charles Dawson Tilly, December 17, 1875. Tragically killed
in the last duel fought at Sand Bar Ferry."

* * *

Earlier Mr. Dunlap had mentioned to his family what a
fascinating history the town of Hamburg, South Carolina,
had. Now, crossing the Savannah by way of the Fifth Street
Bridge, he returned to the Carolina side for evidence of this
"spite" town.

"It seems," Mr. Dunlap began his story, "that Henry
Shultz, a poor German immigrant, came to Augusta in 1806.
He became a boatman on the Savannah and saved money to
buy a flatboat. While he was working this boat between
Augusta and Savannah, he had the idea of building a bridge
across the river. In 1814 he built the Fifth Street Bridge we
just crossed. He and his partners made this a toll bridge, and
he became wealthy almost overnight."

"Wow!" said Phil.

"Next he built a bank, which he called the Bridge Bank,
since it was located near the river and his bridge. This bank

made its own currency—'bridge bills.' Everything he touched seemed to turn to money.

"An old newspaper article I read says resentment sprang up against him among the people of Augusta, who scornfully called him 'the Dutchman.' At any rate, Shultz decided to return to his native Hamburg in Germany."

As Mr. Dunlap wove through the traffic he watched for landmarks that might indicate what he was searching for.

"Anyway, he never got back home. Agreements he'd made had not been put down in writing and in some way his partners forced him to close the bank. Shultz was broke.

"Bitter, he crossed the river to the Carolina side and built a town to spite Augusta. He swore he'd ruin the town that ruined him. So the town of Hamburg was chartered in 1827."

"So that's what you're looking for!" said Mrs. Dunlap. They had all been wondering how this story would end.

"By offering lower rates for everything, he drew off Augusta's trade. By 1835 Hamburg was booming, and Shultz was rich again."

Her father's ability to remember dates had always fascinated Marcy, as she found it hard even to recall the birthdates of everybody in the family. She started to comment on it just as her mother said, "So he did accomplish what he set out to do."

"But the story doesn't end there."

"I like happy endings, Dad," said Marcy. If she were quite truthful she might have added that she'd also heard enough of this Shultz fellow, but she could tell Dad was intent on finishing.

"So do I, Marcy, but in 1853 a railway bridge across the Savannah River brought doom to Hamburg. The railroad instead of the river began to haul freight. With that and the

Civil War, Hamburg failed as a town. Before long Shultz died a penniless man."

With that remark Mr. Dunlap pulled into a station for gas and inquired about remnants of Hamburg. Remnants it was, for now it was less than a ghost town. The Dunlaps did find the old depot sitting down in the valley to the right of the bridge. Much to their surprise, a family was living in it. They saw, too, the hill on which Shultz had built his mansion.

"Poor fellow," said Mr. Dunlap, "even the location of his grave is unknown. Wherever it is, legend has it that he requested to be buried upright with his back to Augusta, the town he hated to the very end."

"How sad," said Mrs. Dunlap.

"Yes," agreed Marcy, who'd inherited her mother's soft heart beneath her adventuresome spirit.

As they started homeward Marcy reviewed their day. They hadn't seen a ferry or a dueling ground—they were no more. And nothing of importance was left of Hamburg. It had been a "wild goose chase" indeed.

But in spite of it all, it had been a profitable day for her father. Marcy was wise enough to know that because of people like her dad, others in the future might enjoy the past.

* * *

That night after the dishes were all done and they tumbled into bed, Marcy realized another summer day had slipped away. She'd come to love this bedroom, with its balcony window overlooking the ravine and the side of the old inn, but tonight her eyes were heavy. Phil would have to hurry to beat her to sleep tonight. She did take time to wonder, though, what people did when the bank that printed their money went broke, like the Bridge Bank did. Tomorrow she'd ask Dad.

"Darn Phil's time!" she thought, "He's asleep already."

She leaned up on her elbows for one last peek out the window. As usual, the night was shrill with insects. Night clouds drifted across the moon and way off somewhere a star fell. Marcy made a wish on it and was just working up a good yawn when she caught sight of the shadow of someone moving outside the ground floor of the old inn. Like the workmen across the street, he wore a metal helmet that caught and reflected the moonlight as he looked up and down the dilapidated area. Whoever he was, he was tall and thin. Now what was he doing there? And at this hour of night? There was definitely something strange about the old part of the inn. But what? Marcy wished Phil were awake. And then, before she knew it, the figure had disappeared into the night and Marcy was fast asleep.

9.
A Time to Dream

Early the next morning Marcy told Phil about seeing the man in the metal hat snooping around the old section of the inn.

"What did he looked like?" Phil asked.

"It was dark and I was looking down on him, but he was tall and very thin." She frowned in thought. "And he was hunched over like a question mark."

"It must have been one of the workmen across the street," Phil said.

"I'm gonna tell Dad."

"No, Marcy, listen—are you game enough to go through with this or not?"

"Yes, but—"

"Okay. Then keep still until we find out what the old man's hiding. That prowler must think he's hiding something too. You know Dad will make us stop if he finds out."

"Well—all right—" Marcy was curious too, but even her

tomboyishness did not make her as daring as Phil.

As soon as their parents left for the library, Phil and Marcy headed for the bridge. From that vantage point they could see the workmen as they moved about on the construction of the new apartment building.

Marcy was secretly glad now that she hadn't waked Phil. For once her brother needed her. This was one mystery she alone could solve. For awhile they sat on the rail of the bridge with Phil asking, "Is that the one? The one next to the work trailer?"

"No."

"How about the one by the crane?"

"No—he's too fat."

"That guy on the crossbeam over there?"

"No . . ."

Sometimes the answers came emphatically, again with hesitation. Finally Phil's exasperation showed.

"Well, Phil, I can't help it. It was night." Marcy was almost reduced to tears.

"Yeah, yeah," he said, jumping down from the bridge rail, which had grown warm in the sunshine. "Next time wake me up, will you?"

"Where are you going?" she asked as he started across the bridge.

"To see if Jerry's in the library." Phil leaned down to pick up a small stone and, straightening up, hurled it into the ravine.

"Tell Mother I'll be right over here," Marcy called, pointing to the edge of the woods just over the bridge. "I'll be making honeysuckle garlands."

Quickly forgetting Phil's disappointment in her for not being able to identify the prowler, she skipped over to the edge of the woods that skirted the other side of the ravine. This was the spot she watched from her bedroom window each night, the place where the moonlight made shadows and the fireflies danced.

Marcy moved just a little way into the growth of tall pines, gnarled magnolias and Carolina cherries. Vines in their colorful summer dresses grew in profusion around her. It was so peaceful here it was hard for her to realize the library was such a short distance away. She sat down on a low, curving branch of a tree and looked about her. Insects hummed in the tall grass and crickets chirped. In a sparkleberry tree nearby a pair of birds warbled as the morning sunlight dappled the tall branches. Far across the ravine she could hear a workman shout above the whir of the machinery and another shout back. But here was a little private world.

Leaves moved slightly as a faint wind breathed overhead and then died. Far above the tall pines she could see little puffs of wind-driven clouds, some of them edged with gold.

A sting on her ankle brought Marcy out of her reverie. Slapping at the smarting, she looked down to find she had one foot in the path of a train of tiny orange-colored ants. She stooped down and watched them as they labored after their leader, scuttling up and down little passageways and over layers of leaves as if frantically driven by something unexplainable. In a way it was lonely here, but Marcy didn't feel lonely. She leaned happily against the trunk of a tree and fell into a sort of happy daydream.

She thought of the young couple whose courtship had caused the railroad to be here. How romantic that was—Miss Pettus was surely right. Her thoughts drifted on . . . Maybe some day a handsome young man would do something as romantic for her.

A humming sound diverted Marcy's attention. Turning, she saw a pretty little ruby-throated bird. Its wings moved so fast as it glided up and down the honeysuckle vine that they made the humming noise she'd heard. Marcy marveled as it stood still or even flew backwards.

"Oh, I know," she said half-aloud, "that's a hummingbird. There's one in Phil's book."

As the bird hummed away, Marcy began breaking off stems of trailing honeysuckle and yellow jessamine. When she'd pinched off an armful of vines, she moved to the edge of the woods and dropped herself to the ground. A soft breeze gently whispered secrets in the grass. Marcy sighed. The loamy smell of earth mingled with the fragrance of honeysuckle in the quiet of the woods.

On the other side of the ravine the sun struck the windows of the sprawling old inn, seeming to set them aflame. From here, too, she had a view of the bridge, in case Phil should return.

Crossing her legs in Indian fashion, she sat weaving the vines into a garland for her neck. It was cool here, but down in the ravine she could see heat shimmering in little wavy patterns above the railroad track.

Almost out of her vision Marcy saw a movement at the bottom of the ravine. Lifting herself up, she could see old Mr. Crowe coming out of the secret door. The sight of him scattered her thoughts like frightened squirrels. She watched as he looked around suspiciously, fumbled with the lock, and let the vines down over the door. Then he started in his crochety way up the ravine. He was carrying a brown paper bag in his hand. Even from this distance his presence made her heart beat faster.

Hurriedly Marcy finished her wreath of flowers and

followed the road to the library. After the cool shadiness of the woods, she blinked against the glaring sunlight.

There were more people in the library than usual, and Mrs. Dunlap was busy at the desk. Her mother looked up as she passed and Marcy gave her a quick wave in exchange for her smile. Holding the garland she'd made close to her, Marcy headed toward her father's nook.

"Hi, Sweetie," her dad said as she approached him. "What have you there?"

In answer Marcy put the wreath of flowers around her neck. The reddish honeysuckle blooms had wilted now, and her lei wasn't as lovely as she'd envisioned it.

"That's nice," he said. "I'm glad you came up. I was just thinking of walking into town. I've been reading about the battle of Aiken during the Civil War, and I didn't even know there was one."

"Where's Phil?" Marcy asked.

"He's with Jerry. Just you and I'll go. Okay?"

"Okay." Marcy grinned. Already she felt better, in spite of Mr. Crowe and the wilting garland. She loved going places with her dad.

After whispering their destination to her mother they were off. While they walked the short distance, her father told her of the battle of Aiken.

"Were many soldiers killed?" asked Marcy.

"The Confederates lost eight and the Federals twelve. But from what I've read, the South—especially South Carolina— thinks the North treated them very badly."

"That's why they call us damn Yankees," Marcy said in a serious tone.

Her father laughed and then became serious again. "The dead from both North and South are buried in cemeteries here. The newspapers said the Daughters of the Confederacy honor them all with flowers on Memorial Day."

In the parkway across the street from the Baptist Church was a monument erected to the dead. Marcy's father took a picture of it, and they crossed to the marker, where he read the inscription aloud. The Confederates had won, it seems, but as her father read, Marcy could scarcely take in all the details of generals, cavalry, and infantry. She did note that this victory had kept Aiken and Augusta from being destroyed.

On the other side of the boulevard graves were shaded by black-trunked old magnolias arrayed with great ivory blooms. Marcy had been in many old cemeteries with her father, and always there was something about them that she couldn't explain. There was an air of reverence here, a kind of hushed respect. It was as if she walked on hallowed ground.

Her dad always said graveyards tell so much about a people, about their battles, their family history, and, of course, their sorrows.

Her earlier mood of dreaminess returned as she wandered among the graves. How different old cemeteries were from the modern ones. Marcy liked to read the incriptions on the stones. Her dad studied history that way, taking copious notes in his little black book, but Marcy liked to dream. She like to make up stories about what the people buried here must have been like. She could tell a great deal about them by what their loved ones had inscribed on their tombstones.

Leaning over a grave she blew away bits of sand and tiny sticks that partially covered the epitaph. Thoughtfully she read:

Dearest One
Thou hast left us

Yet again we hope to meet thee
When the day of life is fled
When in heaven with joy to greet thee
Where no farewell tear is shed.

"Someone must have loved her very much," Marcy thought as she got up to move on. Just then her father called for her to come over to see the soldier's graves. Sure enough, little American flags waved on each marked grave and on the grave of the unknown soldier buried there.

Many of the gravestones were black with age and covered with a greenish moss. Some of them had sunk low into the earth. Passing under the faint lemon fragrance of the magnolias, Marcy's attention was caught by a tiny grave, and she went over to kneel beside it. A rose had been sculptured with pink granite, but it was done with such infinite care and tender feeling that the petals almost seemed to have life.

Marcy felt a tug at her heartstrings. There was no inscription on this tomb, but just below the flower was engraved, *OUR ROSE*. How heartbroken the parents must have been to lose their baby. She'd ask her mother if one day she could put some flowers on the infant's grave.

Marcy and her father spent almost an hour in the cemetery, studying inscriptions and dates and looking at the beautiful stained-glass windows in the old church, before they started back.

A short detour took them by a corner drugstore where they ordered two strawberry ice cream cones. They waited for them at the counter, and when they were ready, walked on the shady side of the street, munching their cones.

Even with the coldness of the ice cream, Marcy felt all warm inside with a pleasant feeling. Her dad was great.

10.
The Secret of
the Inn

Summer days were sliding by like shadows on a pond. There were trips to the library, historical jaunts and visits to old-timers with their dad, and of course, television and an occasional game of battleship. With all of this, not to mention keeping up with Mr. Crowe's comings and goings, the summer was not the slightest bit dull for Marcy and Phil. Every day brought some new delight or discovery.

Of one thing they'd made certain—when Mr. Crowe came out of the secret door and hobbled up the railroad track, he would be gone at least an hour and sometimes longer. Marcy and Phil had watched him time and again and had decided it was on these trips he secured his provisions. Somewhere out of sight down the track there must be a store, for he always returned with a brown paper bag like one from a grocery store.

It was during his trips that Marcy and Phil would again

venture inside the old part of the inn. Even though Marcy was dying to know what the crooning sound they'd heard was and why Mr. Crowe acted so mysteriously, she felt chilled and uncomfortable at the thought of trespassing again.

Today they made certain he was gone. Their parents were sure to be at the library all afternoon, so it seemed the opportunity had arrived to satisfy their curious minds. For Marcy it had come before she'd fully prepared herself. She trembled inside.

Long rays of light played eerily across the old section of the inn as they slipped around the side bordering the boulevard.

When they squeezed through the narrow, splintered opening, fear knotted Marcy's stomach. She tiptoed behind Phil in his futile attempts to find the gaping hole they'd gone down before—the one that long ago had housed an elevator.

"Do we have to go down that way again, Phil?" Marcy questioned, her mouth already tasting like dust.

"That was where we heard the noise, and I'm not sure of getting to it the other way."

Cobwebs and dirt still hovered over the passageway, but they managed to hang onto the musty old ropes and let themselves down through the elevator shaft to the basement floor.

Crouching down and putting their ears to the wall, they listened for all they were worth. Marcy could hear the thudding of her heart, and she secretly hoped there'd be no sound from the other side. What if there really were ghosts here? What would they do? How would they ever be able to get away in this maze of hallways?

After what seemed an eternity of waiting there in the

semi-darkness, a creaking, creaking noise floated to them. And then it began—the low crooning they'd heard before.

In just that short time Marcy's whole world seemed to have changed. Even Phil's red hair looked black as Marcy watched him in the dim light. Like someone in a movie he felt the wall with open palms. running his hands across the panels and tapping them now and then. Marcy's heart still pounded against the wall of her chest as she stood there in speechless misery. This couldn't all be real!

Just as she felt the urge to run for dear life, a door opened. There was no handle on their side and in the faint light they hadn't realized there was a door. Amazed, they saw the shadow of a little old woman appear in the doorway.

"Come in," she called in a syrupy voice that was hardly more than a whisper.

The story of Hansel and Gretel flashed through Marcy's mind. She wanted to run, but her feet were stone. Phil, too, was dumbfounded. So this was what Mr. Crowe hadn't wanted anyone to know! His wife did still live here! But why was he hiding her? Why was he keeping her locked up in this cellar room like a prisoner?

"Will you play with me?" The voice was childlike, innocent and begging.

They looked questioningly at each other, and before they knew it they'd followed her into a room lighted by kerosene lamps that cast eerie shadows around them. Even though there were no windows, it was cool here. The musty odor of the other part of the inn was overpowered by a sweet lilac fragrance.

The little old lady closed the door and with a faraway look about her she said to Marcy, "Why, you're Rose."

"No, Ma'm," answered Marcy in a shaky voice. "I'm Marcy

Dunlap from New York and this is my brother Philip. We're staying at the inn."

"Oh," she said, her face drooping. Just as quickly, however, it brightened as she asked, "Have you been to a party in the great ballroom yet?"

"No, Ma'm—"

Before she could finish answering, Phil nudged her. Marcy knew that meant shut up and she was baffled by the strangeness of it all until Phil whispered, "She's senile—like Aunt Clara."

When she looked at the little woman again, she saw that she'd taken up a doll and sat down in a wicker rocker in the center of the room. Now she was rocking it and smiling and crooning. So this was what they'd heard! As Phil's eyes met hers, Marcy realized that he was right—this little woman lived in the past. Like Great Aunt Clara, whom their mother had taken them to see in the nursing home, Mrs. Crowe was a little child again.

As Marcy watched her sitting there crooning to the old-timey doll, she thought what a dignified, almost pretty picture she made. Her white hair was pulled up and knotted on top of her head. Faded blue eyes looked right past them, and in spite of her wrinkles the paleness of her skin made her head look like grey marble. In fact, her eyes, face and hair seemed to blend together like a figure done by a sculptor.

Marcy's taut knot of fear began to loosen as she looked at the small, dainty face. The tiny features were framed by wispy nylon lace at the throat of her dark dress. She and Phil just stood there trying to take it all in, as Mrs. Crowe sat straight in her chair, rocking, rocking. How tenderly those wrinkled, veiny little hands held the old doll, with its cracks in its plaster head.

While she rocked and crooned Phil and Marcy looked around the room. The smell of lilacs was still strong and sweet. Obviously this room had once been a wine cellar, for the racks where bottles used to be stored were now housing colorful little trinkets, artificial flowers, and many other dime-store souvenirs. On a marble-topped table nearby was a tarnished gilt frame enclosing a picture of a smiling, handsome couple. The girl was beautiful, with short golden curls. Dressed in riding clothes, she sat astride a well-groomed horse and smiled down at the good-looking man holding the reins of her horse. His face reflected her love. Across the bottom corner of the picture was written, "To Lillian with all my love, Your husband, Silas."

"Why, that's Mr. Crowe!" she heard herself say aloud and yet she couldn't believe it was possible. And the lady in the picture had the same sweet face as the little old lady in the rocker. Incredible! But hadn't Mother told them she had married her riding instructor? And that her family had disapproved? Quietly she motioned Phil to come over.

It was impossible for them to take everything in. As the little old woman sat there fussily arranging and rearranging the doll's long white dress, Phil and Marcy continued to look about them. Relics of long ago cluttered the room. Screens with colorful designs divided the area into kitchen, bedroom and sitting room. Marcy could see a two-burner oil stove behind one screen. Cardboard boxes filled with paraphernalia rose like a pyramid in a corner.

An old-fashioned trunk with an oval top sat against one wall. The only sound in the room except for the creaking of the rocker was an antique clock; it ticked with a measured, solemn sound.

Now the little woman got up slowly and looked at the

children as if she were seeing them for the first time.

"Hold my baby," she said to Marcy, "and I'll show you my trunk."

Tenderly she handed Marcy the doll. Its face, with its millions of tiny cracks, held the same expression as Mrs. Crowe's. The doll's round glass eyes stared at Marcy from a perfectly-shaped head and rolled shut in their loose sockets when she cradled the doll in her arms.

If there was ever anything that held more fascination for Marcy and Phil than an old trunk they couldn't think what it was. They stooped to see the contents as Mrs. Crowe eased herself down on a little needlepoint stool by the trunk.

She opened the trunk and took out an old leather Bible with gilt lettering on its worn covering. Holding the back cover that had broken loose she leafed to a certain page. "That tells who I am," she said to Phil. "Sometimes I don't remember, but it's all written down right there for me. Here, read it to me." She turned the Bible toward Phil.

Somewhat falteringly he read the thin, spidery writing, "Lillian Lucretia Pinckney, Daughter of John Robert Pinckney, Jr., and Lucretia Rose Vincent."

A shadow came over her face as she turned to another page. "And this tells of our Rose."

So the tiny grave Marcy had seen in the cemetery was their baby's! A lump came into Marcy's throat. For several moments they all sat motionless until Phil spoke.

"Mrs. Crowe, may I look at this?" Phil was pointing to some stacks of money, and Marcy had never seen him look so surprised before. She knew he'd been itching to see what else was in the trunk. Mrs. Crowe reached down and handed the stack of currency to him.

Phil whistled as he flipped up an end of the bills and let

them shuffle down. He could see the printing now on both sides.

"Say! This is Hamburg bank currency." he cried. Would Dad like to see this!"

"Is it still good, Phil?" Marcy asked agape.

"Not to spend, but for museums, yes."

Mrs. Crowe seemed not to be listening but was occupied with opening a slender, ornately carved box. When she succceeded in opening it, Phil and Marcy gasped. There, right before their eyes, lay a handsome pair of pistols. The single-barreled weapons were polished to a high sheen.

"Dueling pistols!" exclaimed Phil in disbelief.

"Yes," she said, "Before I was born my grandfather was killed in a duel with one of these pistols."

"Oh," said Marcy sadly.

Mrs. Crowe seemed almost natural now as she began the story. Yet her frail voice had a distant quality about it.

"The disagreement was over a strip of land adjoining their properties. Here is the challenge."

From the top of the box she took a yellowed sheet of paper with handwriting so fancy that it seemed unreal. She handed it to Philip and he read aloud.

June 12, 1870

Sir John Robert Pinckney,

I have received your communication of June 5, whereby you state the land along the grey moss oaks belongs to the Pinckney estate. You degrade my character and grossly insult me by suggesting that I would use your land as my own.

68

*In the face of such an affront I challenge you to
meet me in the field. You may have the honor of
selecting the weapons and time for our meeting in
the secluded glade to settle our personal diffi-
culties.*

Drayton DuBois Hampton

"Gee Whillikins!" said Marcy, her eyes sparkling.
"Wouldn't Dad flip over this!"

Hardly able to contain himself, Phil could tell there was
writing on the back of the old challenge. He turned it over,
and there in a feminine hand was written:

*In the prime of life my darling fell a victim to
the barbarous habit of dueling.*

"And this is my grandfather's diary," Mrs. Crowe continued, lifting a handsomely-bound journal onto her lap. "My
grandmother gave me all his personal things." As she sat there
she drifted again into her dream world. After a while she
looked at Phil in a curious way and said, "Well, for goodness
sake, Thomas Marion, when did you check in?"

Phil forced a smile and looked at Marcy. They understood.

They knew, too, that the trunk contained so many more
interesting things they hadn't yet examined—letters yellowed
with age, a tiny gold watch, little trinket boxes, and many,
many more valuable items. It was unbelievable! There was so
much history packed into this trunk that they knew it would
take their dad's breath away. But still, in spite of it all, they
knew they couldn't take a chance of Mr. Crowe's returning to
find them there. Carefully Phil and Marcy replaced the
contents.

69

Already Mrs. Crowe had gone back to her rocker. "He's going to bring me a present," she smiled.

"That's nice," Marcy said, and as she handed her the doll she thought, "Poor thing, she doesn't even realize she's being hidden away." Now Marcy knew that when Mr. Crowe walked up the railroad track, he always brought her a surprise. And all those little trinkets stuck in the wine bottle racks must be the things he brought her. She just couldn't imagine that crabby old man being so sweet to anyone. It was all like a fairy tale.

Quietly they slipped away through the door she'd opened to them earlier, leaving her there, rocking and crooning.

"Kinda gives you a spooky feeling, doesn't it?" said Marcy when they'd gotten a distance away.

"When you're alone with them it does, but you just gotta keep remembering that old age does that to some people."

"Yeah," said Marcy, again thinking of Great Aunt Clara. She had thought Phil and Marcy were her children and Mrs. Dunlap was her dead sister. It was all so sad, but their mother had explained that senile people are happy enough in their dream world and that sometimes it was even a blessing.

As they searched for an exit, Marcy was amazed at how calm she felt. The house wasn't haunted after all! There *had* been a deep, dark secret about Telfair Inn, and she and Phil had discovered it. In a way the inn *had* harbored a ghost—a ghost from the past. And there *had* been a treasure. Not a chest with precious stones or pieces of eight, but nonetheless a real treasure for a historical researcher. Now Phil just had to let her tell Dad!

Marcy's heart was beating fast—not from fear this time, but from joy. She knew how elated their father would be when they confronted him with the news—concrete evidence of all the things he'd been delving into all summer—money printed by Shultz's bank, the dueling pistols and challenge, and so much more. For there was no telling what the old journal held. Still, even as they found their way out, assured that Mr. Crowe was not yet due back, and entered the apartment, there was still the gnawing truth beneath it all—to find those treasures they had trespassed!

* * *

Long after Phil had fallen asleep that night, Marcy lay awake, putting the pieces of the puzzle together in her mind. She had been so furious with Phil and she hadn't gotten over it yet. He still wouldn't consent for Marcy to tell their parents. Now they'd surely tell, Marcy had thought, because if Mrs. Crowe told Mr. Crowe about their visit, the cat would be out of the bag, but Phil had been stubborn.

"No, we can't tell yet, Marcy," he'd said. "Even if Mrs. Crowe says anything, he'll think she's just rambling on. You know how she kept thinking we were someone else."

In fact, Marcy had been so angry with her brother she had said terrible things—things she really hadn't meant to say, and now she was sorry. But when she said she'd just tell anyway and he had called her a baby, it had really set her off. Next time, Phil had told her, he wouldn't let her in on things.

"If we don't handle it right," he said, "Dad'll never get to see those things. You don't think Mr. Crowe will invite him in, do you? And you know Dad. He'd never do anything sneaky, even for his beloved research."

That was what made Marcy so mad—Phil's arguments always made sense—but she wouldn't give him the satisfaction of telling him so.

"All right, Mr. Know-It-All, but I'm not giving you much longer," she had declared.

71

"Aw, drop dead," he had muttered, turning to the wall and falling asleep. His last words infuriated her so she couldn't think of a good retort. Instead she just lay there fuming while he dropped off to sleep.

Again and again her mind returned to the mystery of the inn. So it was Mrs. Crowe she'd seen walking in the ravine with her husband on their first night there. He couldn't walk her in the daytime because he didn't want anyone to know she was there. Why didn't he? Why was her presence such a secret? Surely he must love her to be so good to her, and yet he was such a mean-looking, crabby-acting old man. Just the thought of him made her shiver.

Finally Marcy was able to concentrate on the song of a mockingbird across the ravine. Phil's book said it was the father mockingbird who sang at night and in so many different ways.

Daring to wonder what tomorrow would bring, Marcy finally drifted into dreamland.

11.
Coker Spring

The next morning Marcy had an odd feeling in her stomach. It was as if the weight of the world had shifted and was now on her. She knew that when her parents found out what she and Phil had done, they were going to be in for trouble. Phil knew it too. So why put off telling them any longer? What could possibly happen that would make the situation any better for them? And where was he now, while she was here worrying about it all alone?

Marcy walked out onto the veranda and found the sunlight so beautiful it seemed manufactured. She was surprised to see Phil and Jerry and a tanned girl about her own age with short, dark curls coming across the bridge. The big dog, Shep, ambled along behind them in the warm sunshine.

The girl saw Marcy and gave her a smile that carried over into her dark, earnest eyes. Immediately Marcy liked her, even if she did envy her for tanning so nicely instead of freckling as she did.

73

"Make some peanut butter and jelly sandwiches, Marcy, and you can go to Coker Spring with us. Mom says it's okay." If he remembered their heated quarrel of last night, Phil's cheerful voice gave no evidence of it.

Inside, fixing the sandwiches, Marcy learned that the pretty girl's name was Sarah and she was Jerry's sister, the one Miss Pettus had told her about. She learned too that the pack on Jerry's back contained four drinks which they planned to chill in the icy water of Coker Spring.

The sky was bright blue, with billowy clouds floating above, as the four of them made their way to Coker Springs Road. The sun beat down and Marcy's blouse was sticking to her back as they neared the descent from the paved road into a dirt one gullied by many rains. Uncovered roots groped for life along the edge of the roadbed.

"See," said Jerry, "You can't come down here in a car. The road's all washed out."

Great trees stretched tall around them. Jerry said most of the pale green ones were poplars; the others with the red-brown bark were spicy sassafras. Here and there a vine twisted around the trunk of a towering pine like an octopus and then burst into bloom high in the top of the tree it had conquered.

The woods smelled green and mossy. Honeysuckle thickets permeated the air. Overhanging oak limbs made the spring road seem like another world—one of slender willow trees, trailing arbutus, pokeberry plants and tiny fern leaves that closed when taken from their marshy bed. Even here bamboo sprung up between clusters of Carolina cherry trees and blackberry bushes.

"It's like a park," said Marcy, thinking of one they'd visited in upstate New York.

"Yeah," said Jerry, "but a wild one—they're gonna make it into a real one when there's enough money."

"Picnics won't be as much fun when everybody comes," said Sarah. And Marcy thought that Sarah too must like secret places. Already she knew Sarah was the quiet type. She was as game as any, though, to go through grass where a snake might be—she'd even be the third one, and Jerry said that's the one a snake will bite if he's going to bite anybody. Marcy wondered if their hearts skipped a beat like hers when they passed through a place where the underbrush was thick.

The deep woods had Marcy so entranced that they came upon the spring before she realized it.

"There it is!" said Jerry triumphantly. Marcy could hear the water trickling, but she couldn't see it. The spring bed was covered over with a little house-like construction, but the old bricks were crumbling and broken. Marcy knew the little door-like opening on the front must be the place to get water, but she couldn't see the spring.

"Where's the water?" she and Phil asked simultaneously. Jerry and Sarah laughed.

"Down here," said Jerry, pointing beneath a bed of fern and wild grapevines.

"I don't get it," said Phil.

"This is the horse trail," said Sarah, "and they cemented the spring bed over to make the water run down here into this trough so the horses could drink when the riders came by."

"And Miss Pettus thinks it's outrageous," said Jerry. "She's a Daughter of the American Revolution and she thinks historic spots should be preserved. Coker Spring was the chief source of water around here until 1890."

"And she says," added Sarah, "that if you drink water

75

from Coker Spring, you'll always come back to Aiken, no matter where you roam." Sarah's dark eyes danced as she waved them forward with her hand, "So, drink up!"

Stooping around the noisy little cascade, they cupped their hands and sipped the bubbling, silvery water. It was cool and refreshing. Jerry splashed his face with it and the others copied him. They laughed, momentarily drowning out the bubbling music of the water. All the world seemed filled with pleasantness.

While Shep jumped playfully around them, Jerry and Sarah shared their secret places—it was as if Marcy and Phil were being introduced to special friends. They watched with wonder the surprise of green frogs and spiders when their world was invaded.

They walked a fallen tree that had lost its battle with the earth about its roots. And all the while they romped in this fairyland, Jerry charmed them with his knowledge of the outdoors. He told them the names of the wild flowers and vines, warning them against the dangers of some as their father had done. He chanted the age-old jingle, "Leaves of three, let them be!" He whistled to the birds and they answered him. They all watched while a sweet-singing redbird pulled down his topknot of red over his flat head.

"Say, there's a praying mantis!" said Jerry in a hushed voice.

Sure enough, almost disguised among the leaves was an insect that looked just like a little old lady at prayer. Its two big forelegs were folded meekly under its bowed head, and its body resembled an old-fashioned skirt.

"That's a cannibal insect," said Phil.

"It doesn't eat people, I hope!" said Marcy. Giggling, she and Sarah backed away.

76

"Of course not, silly," said Phil, "but they do eat good insects as well as bad. And sometimes the female mantis even eats the male."

"Hey, be still, you two," said Jerry to the girls, who were still giggling and jumping around behind them. "You'll scare him away."

Quietly they watched while the mantis turned its head in a wide arc, its large compound eyes bulging from its small, triangular head. They didn't see its prey, but quicker than their eyes could follow the long arms of the mantis shot out and the mouth devoured it.

"O-ooh!" screamed Marcy and Sarah, frightening the mantis away.

"Shucks!" said Jerry. "Wish I'd had a mason jar—I'da' caught him for science. You don't see many of them around."

Still in a giggly state, Sarah said, "Jerry and I used to always keep a jar of tadpoles when we were little. We liked to watch them turn into frogs, but Mamma made us quit. She said God made 'em to live in ponds and we should leave 'em there."

Jerry had pulled out a stubby pocketknife and was scraping sapwood from the bark of a sweet gum tree. He rolled it into little balls with the palm of his hands and told them to chew on it and it would work up like chewing gum.

Phil was game. "This is keen!" he said.

Marcy was dubious, even before Sarah said, "Take it from me—don't try it."

Tauntingly the boys chewed, telling them between chomps how much they were missing. But knowing their brothers pretty well, the girls knew they were having a time trying to keep straight faces.

A little farther on they petted some slick horses between the fence boards and hung from the limbs of spreading oaks.

"The only thing you can hang from in New York," said Phil, "is a jungle gym."

"Yeah," chirped Marcy, "policemen patrol parks just to keep kids out of trees."

Jerry smiled. Marcy liked the way his velvety-black eyes lit up before his slow grin crept over his face.

Finally they returned to the spring, exhausted, to kick off their sneakers and plunge their feet in the icy trough. They sat there dangling their feet in the chilling water, laughing at Marcy's expression when her feet touched the slimy, moss-covered bottom. Drifts of willow leaves floated around their wiggling toes. Refreshed, they stepped out on a grassy plot, their feet red and tingly.

Sitting across the fallen tree, they ate their sandwiches and drank their cooled drinks. Then Jerry found a sassafras tree. Whittling away tiny pieces of exposed root, he told them old-timers used it for toothbrushes. Fraying one end, he fanned out the root into soft threads.

"Try it," he said, holding it out to them. "If it's too strong, stick it in the spring." And he began to rub his white teeth vigorously.

The spicy aroma of sassafras filled the air. When Marcy put the root into her mouth, she was surprised to find that it tasted exactly like it smelled. She couldn't tell where smell stopped and taste began.

The sun was low when at last they started homeward, the girls arm in arm behind their brothers. As they trudged up the hill, Jerry carried on a running call with a bobwhite in the thicket. It was almost as if the woods were telling them goodbye.

When they emerged from the valley and the top of the inn came into view, Marcy's wonderful thoughts fell in a heap about her. For a whole day she'd forgotten about the Crowes! If Phil had remembered, he'd made no show of it. If only Phil would let them share their secret with Jerry and Sarah. That would help. After all, they had become such good friends. But she knew he'd never consent. If nothing else, he'd say Shep would be a dead giveaway with his master in the basement of the inn. As quickly as the thought of sharing their secret had come upon her, it fled.

With the promise of many more happy excursions, Marcy and Phil watched until their newly-found summer friends had crossed over the bridge and disappeared from view.

12.
A Terrible Accident

Almost every day for the next week Marcy and Phil slipped in to see little Mrs. Crowe. With more time to explore they found an easier way to get to her basement room than by climbing down the elevator shaft. Even though they were always careful to leave before it was time for Mr. Crowe to return, there was the uneasy feeling that they might get caught. Twice they had narrow escapes, and Marcy vowed she would not go again. Yet when the next opportunity presented itself, she couldn't pass it by.

Sometimes they found Mrs. Crowe cheerful and talkative; other times she would be all alone in her dreamworld. One day she didn't remember having seen them before at all. At first Marcy was confused and upset and they slipped away, but Phil reminded her again that Aunt Clara had been like that too.

Still, the little old lady's memory of past events was

marvelous. So many of the things she told them were right in line with their father's research. And of course Marcy was still dying to tell him. Of one thing she was certain— somehow, some way, he just had to see those historical treasures before they returned to New York. But as usual Phil kept saying, "We will, Marcy, I promise, but we gotta find just the right time and do it the right way."

"You think Dad's going to be mad, don't you?" she asked.

"Well, he won't be pleased that we trespassed."

"We've been downright deceitful, Phil, and I feel terrible about it." Marcy was on the verge of tears.

"Okay, okay. Maybe tomorrow'll be the day."

Again they had talked just before bedtime and the memory of it was still fresh in Marcy's mind as she crawled into bed. *Phil just had to let her tell tomorrow!* Even if they did get punished or have to move, or whatever was to happen, she couldn't keep the burden of their secret any longer.

Although she'd tried to make Phil talk to her some more, he'd fallen asleep without so much as a fleeting thought of planning for tomorrow.

Late in the afternoon a thunderhead had edged toward the sun and spread over it, causing dark to come earlier than usual. Now clouds scudded across a grey sky. Marcy lay with her pillow across the windowsill and breathed the cool night air. It smelled of rain. She had come to look forward to this time of evening. And now she listened as the crickets gave their daily concert, chirping first over here and then over there. Now and then there was a lull, and then they would all start up again together. It was like a choral reading her class had done in school.

Thunder rumbled across the sky and the wind began to

whistle through the bamboo hedge and echo in the ravine. It swayed tall pines into sighing and bent a limb which scraped the inn with a rasping sound. The night loomed shadowy as shutters whipped against the house. Lightning and thunder began to play across the sky.

Suddenly the night exploded. Silver whips of lightning tore at the sky amid claps of thunder; rain slashed against the window. Marcy lay there listening to the pattern of the wind as it rushed the rain in booming torrents, rested it, and rushed it again. She wasn't afraid of thunderstorms. Since she and Phil had been little tots, they had watched them with their father. He'd explained that lightning is just a big spark of electricity that jumps from cloud to cloud or from cloud to earth, and he'd let them make their own thunder by blowing up an empty paper bag and holding it tightly while they popped it.

To Marcy's surprise the downpour stopped as suddenly as it had begun. She couldn't believe it. Slipping her feet over the side of the bed, she pushed up the window she'd closed against the rain.

The sky was somewhat brighter now than before the storm, even though it was after her bedtime. There was a fresh piney odor to the night. Marcy breathed deeply.

Suddenly she caught her breath. From her window she could see the humped shadow of Mr. Crowe moving laboriously near the edge of the ravine. He was holding a flashlight in front of him and trying to straighten out his crooked back in an effort to look up. Was he checking the building for storm damage? Marcy strained to see, leaning out as far as she could without dislodging the screen. She dared not let him see her.

All at once from out of nowhere *the man* was there—the

same one she'd seen snooping before. His hard-topped hat was a silver ball of light in the moonlight. Even from this angle she could tell it was the same man—tall and thin and bent over like a question mark. His awkward gait picking up speed, he rushed toward Mr. Crowe. Angry voices floated up to her and then she saw the man jerk his arm back as if to hit Mr. Crowe. She saw Mr. Crowe raise his cane in the air and then fall to the ground. The workman's hat was a streak of light as he ran down the edge of the ravine.

Terrified, Marcy managed to get to Phil's bed. Shaking him, she called frantically, "Phil! Get up! Quick! Something's happened to Mr. Crowe."

Phil came out of his sleep reluctantly, cross with Marcy for shaking the daylights out of him.

"Th-that man—he came back and Mr. Crowe's hurt—down there." Marcy was almost incoherent in her haste to get Phil up.

"Huh?" He was sitting up now, and what Marcy was trying to tell him was beginning to make sense. "You sure?"

"Of course I'm sure!" Marcy was impatient with his sluggishness. "Come on. Hurry! We can go down the fire escape." Already she was removing the lower screen.

Barefoot, clad in pajamas, they crept stealthily down the rusty iron steps. Bravely Marcy led the way until they stepped in the tall grass where she'd seen him go down. Then she fell back by Phil's side and pointed, shivering, to the spot. Even before they reached Mr. Crowe, they could tell he was motionless.

"Do you think he's dead, Phil?"

Phil opened his mouth to speak, but no words came.

When they reached him, Phil pushed aside the tall straggling grass and the two of them stood there staring down

83

at the old man, now a crumpled heap on the rain-soaked earth.

"Is—is he still breathing?" Marcy's voice was no more than a stammering whisper.

Phil wasn't afraid of him now, but he knew they had to get help. "Run get Dad, Marcy. I'll stay with him. And remember," he added, "don't tell any secrets."

For all she was worth Marcy ran toward the entrance of their apartment. Glad to see the light flooding from the windows of the sitting room, she knew her father was still reading.

Within seconds Mr. Dunlap was by the side of the old man. His presence had a calming effect on the children. As Marcy tried to fill him in on the episode of the snooping workman, he reached down to feel Mr. Crowe's pulse.

"Go wake your mother," he said softly to Marcy. "Tell her to call an ambulance."

The events of the next hour fell so closely behind each other that Marcy did not realize she was still in her nightclothes until the sheriff arrived. After Mr. Crowe had been taken to the hospital and they were assured he would be all right, Mr. Dunlap called the police department to report the prowler.

Still excited, Marcy told of how the man in the hard-topped hat had threatened Mr. Crowe. She hadn't actually seen him hit the old man, but she did see him run from the scene, which she knew always made a person seem guilty. As Phil watched Marcy recount the happenings, she had the feeling he was somewhat ashamed he'd slept through it all. But she also knew he was listening closely to make sure she didn't tell too much.

Pulling his car up close to the ravine, the policeman let the great ray of his searchlight play across the old inn and down into the ravine. Like a huge eye the beam searched for the culprit, but to no avail.

By this time the Fergusons had been aroused and came out to hear the startling news. Even though Mr. Crowe was such an unfriendly person, they too hated to see anyone in trouble. Marcy and Phil, however, had other cause for concern. Who would take care of Mrs. Crowe while he was in the hospital? What would happen to her now?

Giving up their search for the time being, the officers returned to their station. After learning that the prowler had not actually harmed Mr. Crowe but had frightened him into some kind of an attack, the Fergusons and the Dunlaps finally returned to their apartments and to bed.

"Marcy," said her dad as they retired, "that old man actually owes his life to you. If he had stayed on that wet ground all night, he would have caught pneumonia."

Now was the time to tell him, while he was praising her. Marcy felt sure of that and looked at Phil, but the scowl on his face let her know she'd better not.

The minute she and Phil reached their room, she confronted him. "But why not? See here, Phil Dunlap, you're not as smart as you think you are!" Marcy was sick and tired of Phil's promises.

"Now listen here, stupid. We'll have to ask the old man first. Don't you see? It's his secret. We'll just have to slip her food until we can see him."

The argument over telling their secret was pulling her and Phil apart and she couldn't stand it much longer. Marcy wanted to run to her mother and pour out the story, but maybe Phil was right. And yet, the knowledge of it all was like a stone on her chest.

At least she knew now why Mr. Crowe had been so mean—to keep people away so they wouldn't know his wife was there. And children had posed the greatest threat of all, for naturally they were more curious than older people, especially about old houses.

Still the mystery of *why* he was hiding her away hadn't been solved. And the prowler? What was he after? Did he know, too, that she was there? Marcy's mind was still a muddle of unanswered questions.

All she really knew for certain was that that night was the longest of her life. Morning was almost ready to dawn when at last she fell asleep.

13.
A Visit to the Hospital

It was a sleepy Marcy who arose to meet the challenge of the next day. Knowing the anxiety of the previous night, her parents had cautioned Phil when they left for the library to let her sleep late.

Marcy awoke with a start. The thunderstorm of last night had washed the earth into brilliance, leaving diamond raindrops hanging on the leaves. But Marcy's uneasiness overshadowed the beauty of the day. The realization was fully upon her now that she and Phil were wholly responsible for sweet little Mrs. Crowe, for she was *their* secret now.

At Phil's suggestion they made some cream of wheat for Mrs. Crowe and slipped in to see her. Gently they explained that Mr. Crowe was in the hospital, but she was not to worry as they would take care of her. They were relieved to find that she didn't seem to be worried and after her initial "Oh," in which her mouth became as round as her eyes, she moved into her happy dreamworld again.

After their visit, Phil and Marcy made plans to divulge their secret.

"Dad," Phil asked at lunch, "can you get us permission to see Mr. Crowe?"

Mr Dunlap looked up, his face registering surprise. "Well— that might be arranged."

"I don't think so, dear," put in Mrs. Dunlap. "When I stopped by the hospital this morning, the nurse said he'd been most uncooperative."

"That's understandable," said Mr. Dunlap, remembering their first encounter.

"But they're actually having trouble restraining him at times. Unless he's kept under sedation she said he even tries to get out of bed. It seems he suffered a slight stroke that hinders his speech and his ramblings make no sense at all. Do you really think it would be wise for the children to see him?"

Marcy and Phil would know what his ramblings meant, of that Marcy was sure.

"Please, Mom," begged Marcy.

"It's an emergency," added Phil.

Dumbfounded, Mr. and Mrs. Dunlap looked at each other; finally Mrs. Dunlap said, "Well—suppose we leave it up to the nurse on duty. All right, Tom?"

* * *

Within an hour Phil and Marcy were marching behind a white-gowned nurse down the antiseptic-smelling corridor of the county hospital. Speaking over her shoulder, the nurse said, "I'm glad to learn the rumors I've heard about Mr. Crowe aren't true." Her voice was as crisp as her uniform, and yet Marcy thought she detected a trace of a smile.

"Wh-what rumors?" asked Phil.

89

"That children are afraid of him."

Marcy had felt nervous all along about coming in to see Mr. Crowe, and now tenseness grabbed at her muscles. As far as she was concerned, the rumors *were* true, quite true.

"Here we are," the nurse said as she turned into a room. Marcy and Phil followed her. There was no one in the other bed in the room with the old man. He lay deathly still on the high white hospital bed, his ashen face almost as white as the sheet. Marcy's heart sank. His grey head lolled back across the pillow and his thick glasses lay on the bedside table.

"He looks dead!" thought Marcy with an impulse to run. Their panic-stricken flight from him at the inn was fresh in her memory.

The nurse had crossed to the bed and bent over the lifeless form. "Mr. Crowe," she said, "there's someone to see you." Without a change of facial expression the old man grunted and the nurse motioned them to come over.

Marcy's feet would not move. "You go," she whispered to Phil.

"I'll be at the desk just outside if you need me." The nurse had a more cheerful tone as her soft-soled shoes took her to other duties.

Marcy watched as Phil edged up to Mr. Crowe's bed. The old man's expression still had not changed and his eyes were closed.

"M-Mr. Crowe?" Phil called softly.

There was a gutteral acknowledgment.

"It's—it's me, Mr. Crowe. Philip Dunlap, the redheaded boy you chased."

Life came into the old man's face. He opened his eyes and reaching out an arthritic hand groped for his glasses on the table.

90

"You—you don't need your glasses, sir. I—we just wanted to tell you that we—Marcy and I are taking care of her."

There was another gutteral utterance, louder this time as he made an effort to lift himself up. His face looked pained as he tried again to speak. His gnarled hands clutched at the bars on his bed.

"She's all right Mr. Crowe. We took her breakfast, but we can't go on keeping it a secret." Phil rushed on. "We came to get your permission to tell Mom and Dad."

The expression of relief that came over the old man's face was one Marcy would never forget if she lived to be a hundred. Her courage had been building momentarily, and now she stepped up beside Phil.

"She likes us," she said. "We've been playing with her." Marcy was surprised at the calmness in her voice.

The noise that came from the pathetic figure sounded like "Yes. Yes." They were sure of it when he dropped his head back on his pillow. At first Marcy thought he'd fainted, until a look of peace and contentment passed across his countenance. The creases in his face deepened into a smile. When he turned toward them, the look he gave them of joy, of thankfulness, needed no words. Marcy saw a tear roll down his cheek. Her heart went out to him. He'd given the impression of being a hard, tough old man, but he was really soft underneath. He'd been like a mother bird protecting her babies. Compassion welled within her breast.

When they tiptoed out and rejoined their father in the lobby, they couldn't talk fast enough. There was a deluge of excited exclamations and happenings. Mr. Dunlap was so shocked by it all that instead of starting the car he just sat there with his mouth open.

He was interested, of course, in the historical finds, as they most assuredly sounded authentic, but he just couldn't believe all this had been going on without his having any knowledge of it. He really must be an absent-minded professor to have been so preoccupied in his work. Finally he said, "Just wait until your mother hears this!"

They weren't quite as eager to tell their mother, as they knew they were in for a much-deserved scolding for trespassing. But they also knew there'd be no better person to look after Mrs. Crowe than their mother.

All the way back to the apartment they took turns interrupting each other as they filled in the story for their father. When they crossed the bridge and came into view of the inn, Marcy gasped, "It's the razing crew!"

Yellow trucks were parked along the other side of the inn, and men in hard-topped hats moved like ants over the dilapidated area. They couldn't tear the building down—not yet!

Marcy jumped from the car and clasped her hand over her mouth. "That's him!" she shrieked.

"Marcy, whatever is the matter?" asked Mr. Dunlap. He, too, knew the razing crew must not upset Mrs. Crowe until they could make other arrangements for her, but why Marcy was carrying on so he did not know.

But Phil knew. "Which one?" he cried and bounded after Marcy.

"The one who's way out ahead of the others. The one who's shaped like a question mark," she shouted, running toward the inn.

14.
Happy Ending

Marcy was right. The man she had spotted on their return from the hospital had been the one who threatened Mr. Crowe. Marcy's shouts had alarmed him, causing him to run into the wooded area behind the inn.

When Marcy calmed down enough to explain the situation—with Phil's help, of course—matters were taken care of. The other workers quickly apprehended the suspect, as he could not escape across the ravine. As it turned out, he was not a criminal fellow but one whose childish curiosity had not been curbed. He, too, had decided Mr. Crowe was hiding something when he ordered off the razing crew earlier, and he was trying to find out what it was. He readily admitted he had done wrong and would take his punishment, but he insisted again and again that he never intended to hurt the old man.

After the excitement of the moment had waned, Mr.

Dunlap learned from the supervisor that the rubble of the unused portion of the building *must* be cleared this time. The supervisor was shocked to learn that this was the reason Mr. Crowe had been so obstinate about the area before, but he was very understanding. Right away he told his men to move down to the far end to begin dismantling. In the meantime the Dunlaps would make arrangements to move Mrs. Crowe.

Eager for his father to see Mrs. Crowe's historical treasures, Phil led his father below while Marcy ran to the library to get Mrs. Dunlap.

When Miss Pettus heard Marcy's news, her look of surprise became even more so. "A trunk?" she asked, forgetting her library voice. "May I come too?"

As the three of them traipsed over the bridge, Marcy was skipping ahead and talking for dear life.

"Marcy!" Her mother's voice stopped her in her tracks. "You might have been hurt. You and Phil should never have trespassed."

Marcy knew that was just the beginning on that score, but right now everybody was just too mixed up and excited to stay on the subject of discipline.

Miss Pettus was so excited her gait resembled a puppet worked by strings, as she tried to hurry to the inn without actually running.

When they did reach the inn and entered the secret room under Marcy's direction, Mrs. Crowe's little round eyes twinkled with delight.

"Why, this used to be a wine cellar!" said Miss Pettus, noting with amusement how the cubbyholes along the wall were now filled with trinkets and bric-a-brac.

"Poor thing," thought Marcy, looking at Mrs. Crowe, "she probably thinks we're all guests of the inn."

Mr. Dunlap and Phil were already bending over the trunk. Mr. Dunlap just couldn't take it all in—he just knelt there beside the trunk, repeatedly rubbing his hand over his short red hair. He would open his mouth to speak and close it again. Presently he let out a low whistle.

When he did find his voice he said, "I just can't believe it—an unrecorded duel and even the pistols used, money from the old Hamburg bank, a journal by John Robert Pinckney, and memos—my, oh, my!"

Miss Pettus was standing by Mr. Dunlap, looking as if she would surely faint over the findings.

All the while Mrs. Dunlap was talking to Mrs. Crowe in a gentle voice. Marcy heard her say something about a nursing home and Mrs. Crowe said "Oh?" Without looking, Marcy knew her mouth was round. And then Mrs. Crowe said, "Can I sit in the sun?"

"Yes," smiled Mrs. Dunlap, "you can sit in the sun."

The adults were quite pleased to find Mrs. Crowe so untroubled by it all. Her mother was right. Sometimes it was better if old people did slip into a dreamworld. At least Mrs. Crowe seemed happy.

As Marcy and Phil pieced in the whole wonderful story for their captive audience, Mrs. Crowe seemed to be listening. Occasionally she'd mention the name of someone they did not know, perhaps some guest from the inn's gay past.

When Mrs. Crowe had been settled for the time being in the Dunlap's apartment and they were packing some of her treasures for moving, Mr. Dunlap said, "Now there's a real love story for you romantics. Little Mrs. Crowe fell madly in love with her riding instructor and married him in spite of her 'society' background. And evidently his love matched hers, for when she became old and senile he hid her away for fear he would have to give her up to an institution."

"So that's why he was keeping her hidden!" said Marcy as she looked at Phil. She'd never thought of it that way.

"Poor fellow," said Mrs. Dunlap. "He must not have understood senility at all but thought she'd gone insane and would have to be 'put away' if anyone found out. That goes to show," she continued, "that we mustn't judge others hastily. After all, most people who do act peculiarly have reasons for acting that way—often reasons we don't understand."

Miss Pettus nodded her head in agreement. Her eyebrows still had not fallen from their initial height of surprise but remained suspended above the rim of her glasses. "Why, the value of the contents of this trunk alone," she said, "will take care of the two of them for a long, long time."

"You mean they'll sell them?" asked Marcy.

"Oh, by all means," she answered, "when they learn how the world craves such relics of the past. Yes, indeed, there'll be scads of bids from libraries and museums when they hear of these treasures."

Marcy could tell Miss Pettus was having a hard time containing herself, and as for her father, he was still intermittently rubbing his stubby hair and emitting low whistles.

That evening the Dunlaps talked quietly in the sitting room until long after bedtime. With Mr. Crowe's permission, they'd moved the trunk to their apartment where Mr. Dunlap could pore over the contents.

The entire conversation, however, did not consist of treasures from the past. Phil and Marcy got what they had expected—a good lecture for trespassing. Their parents couldn't be too angry in view of the way things had turned out, but never again, they said, did they want to hear of their children so flagrantly ignoring the law. Even if Mr. Crowe had put up the no tresspassing signs as Phil said, they still had no right.

As for Marcy, they needn't worry about her. She'd had enough of exploring houses to last a lifetime.

* * *

Soon after this, Mr. Dunlap had been telling his family how well his research was progressing, even before the fabulous discovery. He could definitely say now that they would be going home to New York soon. In fact, in time for Phil to get in some practice with the relay team and for Marcy to celebrate her birthday with Ellen.

Marcy and Phil thought they'd be happy to hear it, but now they weren't sure. They hadn't wanted to come south and leave their friends, but they'd had such a good time in Aiken.

All the Dunlaps had visited Mrs. Crowe in the sunny nursing home where Mr. Crowe would soon be transferred from the hospital. In short order Jerry, Sarah, Marcy and Phil proved the rumor false that children didn't like the old man. Though at one time Marcy would never have believed it, she had really come to love him. He was always pleased to see them, and the hospital staff said their daily visits had helped more than the therapy he was receiving to regain his speech.

After the town's newspaper ran the story of the historical relics and Miss Pettus told everyone about their beautiful romance that had lasted through all these years, people made new efforts to be nice to the Crowes. They accepted them with open hearts.

A week later, when the Dunlaps packed their station wagon with personal possessions and the fruits of Mr.

Dunlap's research and pulled away from Telfair Inn, they took with them many indelible memories.

Jerry and Sarah's parents had promised them a trip to New York next summer; then Marcy and Phil could show them *their* city—including a ride on a New York subway during rush hour.

As for seeing their other Aiken friends again, Marcy and Phil had no doubt of it—after all, they had drunk water from Coker Spring!

About the Author

A native of Ridge Spring, South Carolina, Idella Fallaw Bodie is beginning her 29th year as an English teacher. She is a member of the faculty of South Aiken High School. Mrs. Bodie attended Mars Hill Junior College, Columbia College, and the University of South Carolina. In addition to her five books, she has written short stories and selected poetry anthologies. Mrs. Bodie is listed in **Outstanding Teachers of America, Dictionary of International Biography,** and **The World Who's Who of Authors.** Idella Bodie is married to James Edwin Bodie, Sr., an engineer in Aiken, South Carolina.